Praise for

Schoenholtz has deftly wc
create a fascinating tale that explores the influence of fate
and family through a slice of 20th century history that's
punctuated by the Great Depression, the Dust Bowl and
World War II. We never escape our roots. But the events of
life batter and build us in our drive to shape our own destiny.
The book is a page turner. I highly recommend it, especially
if you, like so many of us, have a family secret. *~ Lynne Terry,
editor of The Lund Report, former NPR correspondent in Paris
and reporter for The Oregonian/OregonLive*

I couldn't put this book down. At every turn I looked forward
to seeing where "John" would go next. Schoenholtz knows
how to keep your attention and keep you eager for more.
~ Helen Raptis, TV Host of AM Northwest, Portland, Oregon

A compelling story about how we make a life of the bits
and pieces of DNA, decision-making, and circumstance.
The main character's life is shaped by all three. The author
transports his readers into the lives of his characters and their
struggles, plunking them down in the middle of World War
II and other historical events that tested the human spirit.
Schoenholtz is one of those rare storytellers who paints with
words so effectively, the reader becomes lost in the telling of
the tale. I did. *~ Carol Sveilich, author of three books, including:
Reflections From a Glass House: A Memoir of Mid-Century
Modern Mayhem.*

Michael Schoenholtz blends genealogical research with historical fiction as he tracks the mysterious disappearance of his long-lost uncle who forged a seamless new identity to hide his darkest secret. A fast-paced, adeptly told story. ~ *Syril Levin Kline, author of "Shakespeare's Changeling: A Controversial Literary Historical Novel"*

Call Me John is a story born out of genealogical sleuthing into a decades-long mystery about Great-Uncle Isadore Katz, who at 14 walked away from home and disappeared. Using DNA and other records to begin to unravel the mystery, Schoenholtz provides a fictionalized re-creation of his great-uncle's life. He raises questions about the mutability of identity. Yet, the thread that runs throughout is the human yearning to belong and to make our families proud. ~ *Daphne Bramham, columnist for The Vancouver Sun, author of The Secret Lives of Saints*

CALL ME JOHN

A Genealogical Mystery
Based on a True Story

MICHAEL SCHOENHOLTZ

Acknowledgements

With heartfelt thanks and appreciation to:

Louise Runyan, who instigated many of my fictional excursions, questioned the things that made no sense, knew what I meant instead of what I said, and kept my Oxford commas in their places.

Syril Levin Kline, the first person to hear the true story and say, "This really ought to be a historical novel." It's all her fault—she started it.

Linda Forman and Pearl Ulrich for their help in keeping the story authentic.

Carol Joyce, who insisted that I could do it, even when I had my doubts. She helped me to understand which obstacles were real and which ones were illusions.

Eleanor Wildstein, who challenged many of my assumptions about John's story. She played Columbo, saying, "Just one more thing…" when I least expected it.

Susan Shaw Jin, who researched and unlocked several mysteries about life in Colorado in the 1930s and 40s.

And to my beta readers—especially Larry, Carolyn, Decillis, Sarah Mae and Raven Wing who were enthusiastic, honest and helpful in their assessments.

Most of all, I'd like to thank my father Richard, who loved Sam and Minnie, who ate the same chicken soup as Isadore, and who kept his memory alive for all these years.

Table of Contents

Introduction 11

May 1928, Jersey City, NJ. 15

1928–1929, New York, NY 25

September 1929, Pittsburgh, PA 43

November 1929, La Salle, CO. 57

1932, Fort Collins, CO 71

1940–1942, Cripple Creek, CO 83

1942, Southern California. 97

1944–1945, Germany 103

1945, Southern California. 115

1955, Covina, CA 123

1960, Jersey City, NJ. 129

1980, Southern California. 137

Epilogue. 143

About the Author 147

If you tell the truth,
you don't have to remember anything
~ Mark Twain

Every lie requires two lies to cover it up
~ My father

Introduction

My father's uncle disappeared from his home in New Jersey in 1928, at the age of 14. His fate remained a mystery to his parents and his six siblings for the rest of their lives, but his disappearance was not forgotten.

A few years ago, when I began putting together a family tree, my father, Richard, asked me: "Why don't you find out what happened to my Uncle Isadore?" He hoped that I could simply Google his name and find all the answers, but there was no digital trace of him.

Not long afterwards, several people with the same last name appeared near the top of my DNA matches in Ancestry®, but when I looked at their family trees, nothing connected us. Their ancestors were Irish and English, while mine were Eastern European Jews.

Months later, a new person—one of their cousins—showed up on my list. I could see from her family tree that the ancestor they all shared in common was her great-grandfather John Quinn, an Irish-American who died in 1980.

I looked closer. John Quinn's daughter was one of my matches, and her DNA revealed that she was 50% Eastern European Jewish, indicating that she had one Jewish parent. This wasn't consistent with an Irish/English background, and when I asked one of her granddaughters about it, she was baffled.

When I checked to see which of my known relatives this family was related to, it became clear that John was from my dad's mother's family. The large amount of shared DNA suggested that he would have to be a brother of Isadore, if not Isadore himself. But the brothers were all accounted for.

I wrote to John's great-granddaughters again. They told me that his Catholic parents emigrated from Ireland to New York, and died when he was young, but they couldn't find any census, immigration, directory or death records for them. Neither could I.

According to the family trees and my own research, "John" had no siblings. No aunts or uncles. No cousins. No birth records. It was as if John and his parents didn't exist.

The first official document I could find for John was in the early 1930s, when he appeared in Colorado as a farm hand from New York. His birthday was the same as Isadore's, but he was four years older. The odds of these two men sharing a birthday seemed minuscule—one in 365, to be exact.

I reached my conclusions.

Meanwhile his descendants, who were initially interested in figuring out how we were related, suddenly stopped writing after I gently shared my hypothesis about John's real identity. If he had a prior life, it seemed to be unwelcome news to them, and I was on my own.

For the sake of my great-grandparents and my aging father, I pieced together much of Isadore's journey using whatever information I could find for him and the people around him: newspaper clippings, census records, marriage certificates, phone directories, military service, and obituaries. The search was especially complex because of the many unrelated people that shared his adopted name.

In 1980, John Quinn's life ended nearly 3,000 miles from where he disappeared. Incredibly, he lived for years, died and was buried within a few miles of my childhood home in Southern California.

It's entirely possible that my father could have stood face to face with him across the restaurant counter where John worked, and neither man would have had any idea who the other person was. That imaginary meeting was the impetus for writing this story.

At the end of my search, there were so many questions that official records could never answer. Why did he leave home when the rest of his siblings stayed close to their parents for years? How did he survive the Great Depression alone as a teenager? Did he ever tell his wife his true story?

The fictional aspects of his story are the parts I couldn't answer without using my imagination to fill in the blanks.

So if John is watching, I hope he forgives my literary liberties, because this is my way of honoring the two separate lives of one man.

To one family, he was a loving father, grandfather, great-grandfather and pillar of the community. To the other family, he was a troubled teenager: a son, brother and uncle who was lost forever.

May 1928, Jersey City, NJ

"Isadore!"

He was almost asleep when he heard his name, which he'd hated for as long as he could remember. He cringed and made a face whenever his mother called it from the far end of the long and narrow apartment.

"What!"

"Isadore… mph mm mhm phmhhpm!"

"What, mom?"

"Isadore!"

He left his room and stomped down the hall to her kitchen, rolling his eyes. Only moments earlier, he had lain down on his bed with a book in his hands, to try to get a few minutes of quiet time after school. His father, older brothers, and sisters were still at work, so maybe even a quick nap would be possible.

"Set the table! And don't roll your eyes like that."

Minnie Katz, who stood at 4'10", had seven babies in 11 years. She got off the boat from Hamburg in 1906 with three little kids, and then she had three more children over the next three years. Then came Isadore.

He was 14 now, but his nearest siblings, the twins, were already 19. Someone once told him that he was a mistake, and even though his father, Sam, denied it. But the word echoed at moments like this, when his tiny mother shook a rolling pin, squinted her eyes and meant business.

Isadore opened the silverware drawer and gazed at its contents.

His mom was quiet and reserved much of the time, but she had a sense of humor. That's when Isadore loved her the most. He remembered how sometimes she'd have to pull a few quills from a whole kosher chicken, and deal with the feet. One day she appeared behind him with a chicken claw in her hand, and chased him in circles around the kitchen and the hallway, making clucking noises as he shrieked and laughed in mock terror.

Her humor wasn't evident today. In fact, since Isadore started having trouble in school, she seemed more impatient and cranky with him.

Isadore didn't really know his parents very well. Minnie and Sam spoke Yiddish when they didn't want the kids to understand them, which was rather often.

They came from the old country, emigrating after years of danger and upheaval, including the looting and burning of their villages. They didn't discuss it much, and if Isadore asked too many questions, he would get a response like, "Why do you want to know? Are you writing a book?"

"It's best that sleeping dogs should lie down, and you should leave them alone," his father would say with a thick accent.

In the early 1920s, Sam and Minnie, along with their three girls and four boys, crowded into three bedrooms in a walk-up 4th floor apartment in Manhattan. It was noisy at all hours, and always too hot or too cold. The bathroom was down the hall and shared by several families.

In 1925, they moved into a two-story brick duplex on a quiet street across the river in Jersey City—the place they now lived in. A large bay window framed with potted ferns faced the street.

The house had a stoop outside the front door, and the family would sit on the steps on warm summer evenings. A music teacher lived upstairs with his family, and a Chopin piano concerto could often be heard throughout the neighborhood after supper.

While this was a huge improvement over the place in New York, there were still eight people living at home, even after the oldest daughter got married and moved out. The only bathroom had a line in the hallway at all hours. It didn't matter how urgently a person needed to go; a position in line was rarely negotiable.

"Stop daydreaming. Your father will be here any minute. Set the table," Minnie reminded him. "Go. GO." She shooed her hands toward the dining room.

Sam Katz, a quiet good-natured man with a perpetual grin, worked 50 hours a week making hats. Every evening before he got home, Minnie scurried around to get supper ready.

As Isadore placed the dishes, he paused for a moment to inhale the scent of his mother's chicken soup, as only she knew how to make. Leafy celery tops were the secret, he was once told.

His brothers and sisters arrived one at a time, in a continuous procession of jackets and shoes at the front door. The noise level reached a crescendo just before everyone started eating.

Sometimes they ate in shifts, but Isadore's older brothers and sisters always dominated the dinnertime conversation, no matter how many were seated. Everyone had a story to tell but him. By the time he was 14, he was the only one still in school. The rest of them all had jobs and careers, girlfriends or boyfriends, and lives of their own.

Everybody was gone all day except for Isadore and his mother, and she was usually in the kitchen. The neighborhood had no children left, and his handful of school friends lived too far away to visit unless he took a bus.

His life was boring in his estimation, and he was tired of being treated like a baby and a slave.

His oldest sister, Lil, was already married and had two babies. They came over all the time, as if there weren't already enough people at the table. Now his little nephew, Richard, was the center of attention, and Isadore felt even more invisible at mealtime.

Isadore Katz would sometimes go through an entire meal without saying a word, just to see if anyone noticed. They never did. With everyone talking at once, the conversation merged into a chaotic orchestra of voices that was impossible to join, let alone to comprehend.

Richard and his two aunts, 1928

There were 12 people at the table tonight. Isadore looked around, studying everyone's face. His brothers usually spoke about cars, sports, politics and jobs.

At one point, someone brought up President Calvin Coolidge, and everyone groaned in unison. Isadore saw an opening and interjected, "Hey the Rizzis next door just got one of those new Plymouths." His brothers looked at him for a moment. He had gotten their attention.

Just then, his youngest sister, Jean, knocked over a glass of water, making everyone jump up as the water crawled across the tablecloth. That was the end of that discussion.

After the mess was cleaned up, his three sisters discussed what sounded like female topics, little of which made any sense to him.

It was no use trying to figure out which conversation to join.

Sam was in the middle of a rant about how his generation didn't get to choose careers. They only needed to put food on the table, no matter how it was done. He pointed his finger at Isadore and said, "But God willing, he should grow up to be a somebody rather than a nobody."

Everyone stopped talking for a moment and looked at Isadore, whose face turned red. Then, just as quickly as it went quiet, the hum of conversation resumed.

Tonight felt more hopeless than most, and he briefly wished he could just disappear, but baby Richard kept smiling at him, so it was hard to hold on to that thought for very long.

Occasionally, during the continuous gesturing at the table, Isadore would make eye contact with one of the twins—his bespectacled brother and roommate Willie. He was a 19-year-old engineering apprentice, and the next youngest male in the house. As Isadore's favorite sibling, Willie didn't look past him the way the others did, but they didn't talk often enough. The age gap was too large. They mostly just snored at the same time in the same room and passed each other in the hallway.

Isadore's brother Willie

Late last year, Willie had taken him to a New York pool hall. Sam and Minnie wouldn't have approved, so Isadore was sworn to secrecy, which made him feel trusted and grown up. He sat and watched his big brother play that day, but before they left, he got to play a quick round of pool with Willie when the place was almost empty. Winning was surprisingly easy, and Willie vowed to take him back one day, but he never did. School and work soon consumed him, and eventually they both forgot about it.

This particular night, Willie stopped Isadore in the hallway after dinner. He'd noticed that Isadore was even quieter than usual.

"Hey. How's school?"

Isadore looked down and started to walk away. His older brother grabbed his shoulder and stopped him. "So? How is it?"

"You wouldn't understand," Isadore said, pulling away again.

"Try me."

"Did anyone ever give you a hard time for being, you know…"

"Being what?" Willie asked.

"Did you ever get called a kike?"

Willie sighed. "No. Just 'Jew Boy.' But don't let it bug you, kid. It's just a fact of life."

"I'll bet they didn't spit on you," Isadore said, feeling a bit nauseous as he relived what happened.

"Wait, what?"

"One day last week I was out front, and some guys cornered me, and one of them hocked a loogie on my face, and called me a kike."

Willie's eyes opened in surprise. "Who did this?"

"Some guy. Frank Duffy. It doesn't matter. But every day since then I hear someone clearing their throat like they're going to spit, just to yank my chain. And then they all laugh. I've had it. I hate it. Really. I hate everything." Isadore waited for a reaction from his brother.

Willie knew that school was going to be tough for Isadore. He certainly wasn't the only Jewish kid in 8th grade, but he was short and skinny for his age, and most of his clothes were hand-me-downs from his taller brothers.

Suddenly someone yelled, "Hey Willie. C'mere!" from the dining room. Willie mumbled something and was gone. The end of another discussion.

There was laughter in the other room, and Isadore stood alone in the hallway, looking at a family portrait taken when he was about seven. In this image, he was tightly wedged between his mother and father, almost like an afterthought. If he wasn't there, then they wouldn't have been so squished. There would be more room at the dinner table. And one less person to wait in the hallway outside the bathroom. And no one to spit on at school.

It was all clear. Isadore was only 14, but he could see what lay ahead. Staying at home until he got married, then bringing the wife and kids over for dinner with these same people. All the time. For the rest of his life. And then he'd die. Possibly of boredom.

The next day he walked down Hudson County Boulevard to Public School 34. Climbing the steps to the main entrance, Isadore heard a voice call out behind him.

"Hey look! *It's a door!*" Several boys cackled and snorted in unison. Frank Duffy cleared his throat, as if getting ready to spit.

Isadore snapped. Turning around without thinking, he kicked Frank squarely in the balls, hitting his target precisely. Frank doubled over in pain, and the group quickly knocked Isadore onto his back and took turns punching him until he was covered in blood and mud.

The school bell rang, and everyone, including a handful of onlookers, disappeared into the building.

When he stood up, Isadore saw Frank and the others peering out the window of the front door. He couldn't go to his class looking like this, but the thought of going home, explaining everything to his mother, and then being made to come to school again tomorrow was too much. He just couldn't do it.

After dabbing at his face with a hankie, he started walking north along Bergen Avenue, with no agenda or destination in mind. It began to rain, which washed the rest of the blood away from this face. His stomach hurt from being kicked.

Pausing at Fulton Avenue for a moment, he could see his house with the bay window. There were a few guilty ideas about going home, but they passed quickly and he kept walking. It was still morning, and he could always go home later.

Later that evening, there was an empty seat at the Katz's dinner table. Minnie was peeved, but said nothing. Isadore's sister Shirley asked where he was, and Minnie answered, "He's late."

His plate sat empty on the table. She would deal with him later.

It wasn't until the next day when the school called that she realized he was wasn't coming back.

1928–1929, New York, NY

Isadore kept walking until he was well beyond Fulton Avenue. The leafy residential area transitioned to apartment buildings and then to commercial buildings, but he hardly noticed. A queasy combination of fear and determination ran through him as he stared blankly at the sidewalk passing under his feet.

After about 45 minutes, he arrived at Journal Square, a busy hub of traffic, buses, cars and shops with neon lights. Isadore found a bench outside the bus terminal and gathered his thoughts.

His pocket held a dollar-something in loose change. To the left were the tops of the buildings across the river in Manhattan. The rain and wind had stopped, the sky was clearing, and the smell of bus fumes was getting stronger. This wasn't the way he wanted to spend his afternoon, so he checked the bus fares. The coins in his hand were more than enough for a round-trip ticket to New York on the Public Service bus line. It was a school day, but today he was playing hooky. If he felt like coming home tonight, the last bus back to Jersey City left at 9pm. He'd be in trouble, but it would have been worth it.

Isadore hopped on a blue and red bus at about 10 am, and less than 5 minutes later, he was gliding under the Hudson River through the newly opened Holland Tunnel.

A young girl across the aisle stared at him with revulsion until her mother told her it's not polite to stare. When he touched his puffy face, he realized that he probably had a black eye. Brushing his wet hair back with his hand, he looked out the window, but he could still watch everyone in the glass reflection.

After a few minutes, he hopped off the bus and stood once again in Manhattan, his childhood town. The sounds of honking cars mixed with ship horns from the Hudson river docks. Steam rose from the tops of the tall buildings, like smoke stacks on a ship. No matter how many times he went to this part of Manhattan, he couldn't help but look up.

But Isadore was now a tourist. No more walking behind his family. The decision about lunch was all his, and he didn't have to listen to everyone else's opinion. There was no obligation to be anywhere. What he felt most now was freedom. Still dripping wet with a black eye and a torn jacket, he was on his own, and it was exhilarating.

Around the corner there was a Horn & Hardart automat. Perfect. The place appeared to serve everyone, no matter their status. Customers could pull their own plates of food out of a wall of little windows. There was no need to be served by a snooty waiter, and he was getting hungry. Isadore grabbed a tray, dropped a nickel into a slot, pulled the glass door open, and took out a hot dish of baked beans.

The table was all his, and he felt twice his age. These were the best baked beans he had ever eaten in his life. And there were little bits of smokey meat in it. They might have even been bacon, which he never had at home. His parents would be aghast if they knew. A smirk appeared on his lips as he pictured his mother's face.

Then he went back to the windows and got a plate of mac and cheese. "Hah!" he said out loud, barely containing his excitement. *Mixing dairy and meat in the same meal. Wait a minute—dairy and pork! Even better! Most definitely not kosher.* The smile on his face got wider.

Isadore's stomach was nearly full, but he was having too much fun. He got up and bought a cup of coffee, dispensed automatically out of a brass dolphin mouth, in precisely the right amount. He had never tasted coffee before because his parents always drank tea. A quick trip back to the dispenser to add a lot of cream and sugar, and all was good.

On the way back to his table, he grabbed a slice of apple pie, which he gobbled quickly. The entire meal cost him 30¢, and he was as full as a 14-year-old boy could be.

The place was getting busy, and people were eyeballing his table, so he got up and walked outside. *Where to go,* he wondered. The day was all his.

Above his head were the unmistakable sounds of a cue ball smashing a rack. There was a sign: Julian's Pool Hall, right above the automat. *What the hell,* he thought. Climbing up the stairs and past the "Ladies Invited" sign, he strode into the main room with his chin high. The cigar smoke was thick, even though it wasn't very busy.

The proprietor took one look at Isadore and said, "Hey. No kids allowed."

Isadore turned his black eye to the man, furrowed his brow and said, "I'm not a kid. I'm 18."

The man thought about challenging him, but the phone rang and he got distracted.

There was a voice behind him. "Kid. I'll play you. Two out of three."

A rough-looking guy with slicked-back hair and an unlit cigarette dangling from his mouth had just asked him to play pool!

As the man lifted his right hand to light the cigarette, Isadore noticed it was covered with what looked like a huge ugly burn scar.

Isadore had only played pool once in his life, last year with Willie, and he beat him. Feeling cocky, he nodded his head.

"Okay." They flipped a coin. The tough guy racked the balls, and Isadore began the round with a strong break.

"Two bits," the tough guy said.

"Huh?"

"I've already paid for the hour, but we're betting on the best of three, got it?"

Isadore slid a hand into his pocket. He still had about 35¢. Damn—25¢ for a couple of rounds of pool. He placed a well-worn Liberty quarter onto the edge of the table, next to the one the guy had just set down.

Isadore lost the first game, but not by much. Then he got lucky and won the second round after his opponent scratched the cue ball.

The third time was going to decide who walked away with 50¢. It went quickly, and Isadore easily won. It almost felt too easy.

"How about another round? Let's make it a buck this time."

Isadore only had 60¢ left, including his winnings. Besides, there were other things he wanted to see beyond the inside of a pool hall before he went home to New Jersey that night.

"I don't have a dollar."

"Oh, come on. Gimme a chance to get my money back," the guy said. "What's your name?

Isadore hesitated and then latched onto the first name he could think of. "I'm John. Call me John."

"Gus. Hey how old are you? You're not 18, are you."

John felt a bit of panic, but didn't show it. "Yeah, I am. I just look young for my age." The bruises and his black eye lent some credibility to his story.

"Look, I'll front you the money," Gus offered.

"But I have no way to pay you back if I lose."

"If you lose, you pay me 50¢, and maybe I forget the other 50¢. OK?"

"OK—best of three," John agreed. They played another two games, and John lost both times.

"You owe me a buck," said Gus as he lit a cigarette.

"But you told me.."

"I said *maybe* I forget the other 50¢. So I changed my mind, chump. Pay up." Gus grabbed John's lapel.

"But.."

Gus raised his fist like he was going to hit him, and then he took a drag off the cigarette and blew the smoke in John's face.

"Say, I have a little errand I need done. Do it right and I'll forgive the loan. Screw up and you'll have a matching black eye."

John couldn't believe how stupid he was. *What did I just agree to do for 50¢?*

He should have left while he had the chance, but now he had no choice. Gus was three times his size, and he'd be no match for him.

"OK. What do I need to do?"

John left Julian's pool hall, turned left, and then left again onto Canal Street. Counting to himself: One, two, three blocks, on the right side, some place named Donahue's. Tell them Gus sent me.

The man behind the counter reached into a cash drawer and handed him an envelope. His hands were trembling. John slid it into his coat pocket like he was told.

"That's it? Really?" John thought to himself, as he walked past two cops who were standing outside. They looked directly at him, but didn't say a word. There was probably money in the envelope, which felt thick.

John went back to the pool hall and handed the envelope to Gus, who sat down in a dark corner and quickly counted the cash. When he came back, he gave John two dollars.

"Here, kid."

John slid the shiny coins into his pants pocket. "It was nothing."

"What did you notice on the way to and from Donahue's?" Gus asked.

"What do you mean?"

"Tell me everything you saw."

"Well, there was a grocery guy with a push broom on the corner of Varick and Canal, sweeping old lettuce leaves into the gutter. A hot dog cart at Canal and 6th. There were three ladies standing in front of La Bella Ferrara bakery, speaking in Italian. There were two cops almost in front of Donahue's. They weren't talking. They were looking up and down the street."

"Tell me about the cops."

"OK. One of them was pale and fat, with grey hair. The other one was tall and skinny and had a long face. He was probably about 30. They looked right at me, but didn't say anything."

"Very good. Those are my guys."

John nodded as though he understood, but he wasn't sure what Gus was talking about.

"Say kid, can you whistle?"

John nodded his head, still confused.

"You want to run another little errand for me? You gotta be there by two o'clock."

This time, John needed to be the lookout for a liquor delivery to the backdoor of a speakeasy. His job was to stand at an intersection and do a bird whistle if a new black Ford coupe with two men approached.

Taking his position, he watched the alley around the corner from the establishment. John held his breath as he saw a black car approaching with two men inside, but it kept going straight. Suddenly, the car swung around and came back, turning into the alley. John whistled, and he could hear the delivery truck tires squeal as it took off. It was gone just before the guys in the Ford could see it. John had prevented a bust.

Gus soon appreciated the value of having an observant, reliable, scrawny kid around, whether or not he was 18.

"You got a place to stay?" Gus asked, as he gave John three more silver dollars.

John decided that afternoon to not go home—at least not yet. He could think up some excuse to tell his parents after he made some more dough. These guys were obviously part of a gang, but he knew better than to ask questions.

Over the next 24 hours, he had made enough cash to rent a room in Hell's Kitchen, even though he would hardly spend any time there during the next few days. His errands could be day or night. John ate in the automat whenever he could, and never got tired of it. It was heaven.

Across the river in Jersey City, Sam and Minnie couldn't figure out whether Isadore had run away, or if he had gotten into some kind of trouble. Willie told them what Isadore said about being bullied in school, and being fed up.

MISSING YOUTH, 14, SOUGHT IN JERSEY CITY

State and local police in North Jersey Counties have been notified to look for a missing Jersey City youth, who was last seen on the streets of that city on the morning of May 21st.

The missing boy is Isadore Katz of Fulton Avenue. He is described as being five foot seven inches tall, with brown hair and blue eyes. He wore no hat, but had on a grey overcoat, checkered sports sweater, blue trousers and black oxfords. He was a student at P.S. 34. No reason could be ascribed for his disappearance.

Just in case of foul play, Sam filed a missing person report with the police department a few days later. Still, everyone expected that Isadore would be back as soon as the novelty wore off. After all, how far could a 14-year-old kid get without any money?

Several weeks went by, then several months, and then it was 1929. Jewish, Italian and Irish crime families were competing for bootlegging business during Prohibition. Al Capone was rumored to be the man behind the killings of Bugs Moran's Irish gang in Chicago. Tensions and paranoia were running high.

Meanwhile, John had built a reputation of being dependable and smart. Every morning at 8, he would show up in front of Julian's and get the day's orders from Gus. If any of his errands were dangerous, he didn't know it. Mostly bootlegging-related stuff; running errands and being a lookout. Just pay attention, don't get caught and don't ask questions. Easy rules and easy money. They apparently liked him.

John avoided whiskey, laughed at all the jokes, and nodded knowingly when the talk turned to sex.

Two women of questionable character came in one evening and joined the men at the card table in the corner. One of them was practically in Gus' lap, while the other one looked John up and down and winked at him.

"Which one do you want, kid?" Gus asked. The question caught John off guard, and his eyes widened.

Gus grinned. "What, you ain't never had a girl before?"

John stammered. "Yeah, I have. Plenty of times."

Nothing could be further from the truth. He was still 15, and the girls he had known in eighth grade were only interested in older boys.

"This one's on me. Take your pick, John."

The choices terrified John. The women were older, wore a lot of make-up, and weren't at all what he envisioned for his first time. Before he could respond, the younger of the two women grabbed him by the collar and dragged him into a back room.

"So your name's John? I know a lot of guys named John," she laughed. "I'm Lulu." She snapped her gum. "Come on. What's it gonna be?" She pulled off her blouse.

John turned white. "Can we just talk?"

"Honey, I don't care. You got 15 minutes however you wanna use it. Knock yourself out."

John sat there, unsure what to do.

Lulu rolled her eyes and sighed. "Why, you're just a kid, aren't ya. Too bad. You're sorta cute."

"Look, Lulu. No offense."

She winked at him, pulled her blouse back on, stood up, grabbed her boa, blew him a kiss, and started to rock her embroidered hips out the door.

"Wait a minute, Lulu." John had second thoughts.

Ten minutes later, he walked back into the pool hall. Gus raised his eyebrows. "So?"

John shrugged and grinned smugly, like someone who had just figured something out.

A couple of weeks later, around lunchtime, Gus asked him to come upstairs. They went through a set of swinging doors and Gus nodded at a guy who was standing in the hallway. A door opened, and there was a ruddy square-faced man sitting at a card table, smiling. The door closed behind them. An electric fan hummed from the corner.

"John, I'd like you to meet Mr. Duffy."

The man stood up and extended his hand to John. A gold ring adorned his pinkie finger. "Pat Duffy. How ya doin."

John heard a bit of an Irish brogue, and got the sense that he was meeting a boss, but Gus never mentioned his name before.

Is he the boss-boss, or just a boss? This guy looks too young to be a boss-boss, but look who's talking, John thought to himself.

As he shook the man's hand, he had to think quickly about a last name. Katz wasn't going to work. He had blue eyes and light brown hair, as did his parents and siblings. He could probably pass for Irish.

Oh shit. Here goes. "John O'Brien. Pleased to meet you."

"I hear you've been doing some good work for us. I wanted to see you face-to-face. Where do you come from?"

John cleared his throat. "Jersey City. Sir."

Gus and Pat looked at each other and laughed. "That's very nice. I mean, where are you FROM. In Ireland. Your family," Pat pressed.

The blood drained from John's head. This was going to have to be good.

"Uh—I don't really know. My parents died when I was little. I grew up in a foster home."

"Don't you have any relatives?"

"Nope."

"Hey, my nephew Frank goes to school in Jersey City. PS 34. Maybe you know him."

"Frank Duffy? Jersey City's a big city," John replied, not answering the question. This man's nephew was a painful memory for Isadore. Of all the people to meet in New York, he had to meet Frank Duffy's uncle. John wanted to disappear.

Three shots of over-proofed whiskey appeared in front of the men. Gus and Pat slammed theirs down, while John stared at his glass for a moment, picked it up and raised it to his lips. *How bad could it be?*

After downing it in one gulp, John winced as the whiskey burned a hole in his esophagus. He wondered if it might make a return trip. His cheeks turned red as the men studied his face, their eyes squinting like they were waiting for the other shoe to drop. They leaned back and away from the table. John's stomach was fighting to push its fiery contents back up, and it took every ounce of strength to hold it down. He tried to play it cool.

"You want another one?" Pat offered.

"No, thank you. No, sir."

John was just about to win his battle with the whiskey, when a plate of sardine sandwiches was delivered. The tails hung limply over the bread. "Eat up," Pat said, while taking a bite. He talked with his mouth open, and John could see the fish being ground up between his crooked teeth.

The bile rose in John's mouth. "I need to use the toilet," he said, jumping up and heading for an open door that he prayed was a bathroom. He almost didn't make it. The door slammed behind him barely in time, and the two men heard him lose his whiskey. There was chuckling outside the door.

When John came back, it was all business. Gus had left for a few minutes to run an errand.

"Listen, John." Pat leaned in and spoke quietly. "Someone in the clan is setting me up. It's someone close to me, but I don't know who it is. I need someone who isn't tainted, who doesn't know anyone, who no one else knows. You understand what I'm saying?"

Pat explained that every week at least one of his deliveries had to be called off because the cops were right around the corner. Someone had been tipping them off, and he wanted to get to the bottom of it.

John would help find out whoever was behind the betrayal, and he wasn't to mention a word about it to anyone. Then Pat asked where he lived, which seemed odd.

A few days later, as John approached his apartment, Pat was sitting in his car out front with the window rolled down.

"Hop in. We got some work to do."

Pat confided that he suspected who the bad apple was, but he wouldn't name names. Not yet.

"We're going to Jersey. I'm gonna catch 'em red handed with the paperwork. And I'm gonna need some help afterwards."

They drove through the tunnel into Jersey City and parked down the block from the warehouse where the liquor orders were filled. They waited and watched.

After an hour, two guys pulled up and parked in front of the warehouse, unlocked the door, and used a flashlight to look for something in the office.

Pat got out of the car. "Wait here. I'll let you know when to come in."

"You want me to come in with you now?"

"No, kid. You'll just be in the way. Wait outside. Make yourself scarce. We'll have a little chore afterwards."

Pat snuck into the warehouse through a side door.

John walked halfway down the block and crouched down behind some stacked crates. Gus had given him a .38 revolver weeks earlier, which he groped with his hand for reassurance. He never needed to use it, and wouldn't know how, even if he did.

Suddenly he heard breaking glass coming from the office. There was shouting, and the flash of a gun. One man dropped to the floor while Pat and the second man came running out the front door. They wrestled on the ground. A gun went off twice, three times, but the men continued to wrestle.

A single floodlight made the figures into silhouettes as they fought in front of the door. John heard Pat cry out. He was clearly in trouble. John took a few steps toward the men, pulled his gun out, and tried to figure out who was who. He could see Pat pinned to the ground. John aimed the gun at the other man, and holding it with both hands, shot several rounds while the men rolled around on the pavement.

After the third shot, the fighting stopped, and an eerie silence washed over the scene. A dark figure jumped up and ran along the row of loading docks, his footsteps gradually fading away. John approached slowly and knelt down.

Pat lay on the ground, face up, his blood mixing with a rainbow slick of oil into a puddle on the asphalt. His eyes were half open. His lips tried to mouth something repeatedly, but he choked on his words, and then he stopped breathing.

John looked at the gun in his hand and realized that he had accidentally killed his own boss.

He stood up and paced in circles, muttering, "Fuck. Fuck. Fuck. Oh my God. I killed him," until he realized he needed to get back to his apartment quickly, so that everything looked normal. The walk to Journal Square was about half a mile, and then he hailed a taxi back to the city.

The apartment was noisier than usual, and sleeping was nearly impossible. A drunkard banged into some trash cans under his window and brought an end to his 20 minute nap. John lay in bed thinking.

Did anyone know I left with Pat? Did anyone see us? How long before they discover the body? Did I touch anything in the car?

Maybe I should just act surprised, like everyone else. No one would know I was with Pat, right?

Just before 8 am, he headed down toward Julian's Pool Hall, like he always did. Turning the corner, he saw Gus standing in his usual spot, only this time, he had the two bad cops with him. As soon as Gus saw John, he pointed, "There he is!" and they all started running towards him.

John turned around and ran as fast as he could toward uptown. A quick glance over his shoulder showed that the men were gradually falling behind.

At the Spring Street subway station he ran down the stairs, two at a time, hopped the turnstile and took the E train to Penn Station. When he got off, he quickly got lost in the chaotic crowd of morning commuters in the main lobby.

The first train on the departure board was Pittsburgh PA, leaving in four minutes. He nervously stood at the ticket counter, while someone in front of him searched for exact change as though they'd never seen American money before. His eyes scanned the room, but he didn't see Gus or the cops. Scarcely able to catch his breath, he bought a one-way ticket and then sprinted to the track just as the doors closed.

John didn't stop panting until the train was out of the tunnel and rolling through the grey industrial landscape of Elizabeth, New Jersey.

The memories of the last 12 hours replayed in a graphic loop, even with his eyes closed.

I'm a wanted murderer. I can't ever go home. They'll find me.

* * *

Only a few miles away in Jersey City, Isadore's bed was freshly made and his desk sat untouched just as he had left it. It looked as though he had stepped away for a few minutes. It was too painful for Minnie to be in the room for more than a change of bedding once a month and a quick sweep. Sam wouldn't set foot inside.

September 1929, Pittsburgh, PA

In late September 1929, John O'Brien was almost 20. Isadore Katz was almost 16.

Downtown Pittsburgh struck John as sort of an imitation Manhattan. It was much smaller, a lot smokier, and downright dreary. He wondered if maybe this wasn't such a great idea, but it's not like he had time to choose a better city.

He had gotten into the habit of carrying cash with him, as he didn't trust the lock on his apartment in New York. Having a wad of money in his pocket took some of the pressure off finding a job right away.

Cheap apartments were easy to come by in Pittsburgh, especially in converted hotels. The Atlas offered weekly rates, and once John got past the overly nosey landlord who wanted to know how old he was, he rented a unit that was decorated with stained floral wallpaper and had its own sink.

The window looked over the top of an awning that was covered with flashing lights. Downstairs was a Chinese eatery.

I wonder if they have baked beans. Probably not.

After walking around downtown and buying a few necessities, John picked up a newspaper and walked past the restaurant and its bright signs.

The Paris Inn…Special Dinner $1.25, Dancing. What kind of a name is that for a Chinese restaurant?

He entered the side door of the hotel, walked up the stairs and settled in for the night.

The noise from the restaurant got louder and rowdier as the evening wore on. There had to be bootleg liquor someplace down there, John concluded. Either that, or Pittsburghers didn't get out very much, because they were having a lot more fun with Chop Suey than anyone should.

Laying in bed with the Gazette, John made a mental inventory of his marketable skills, but came up with nothing. Keeping an eye out for cops probably wasn't what most employers had in mind.

The Male Help Wanted ads weren't very encouraging:

Experienced Window Trimmer. *Nope.*

Christmas Card Salesman. Tissue lined envelopes. Gold lettering. *Hah!*

Chippers, White or Colored, Experience in Steel Foundry Chipping. *Nope.*

Ambitious Men. Why not engage in a profession worth of your best effort. Mutual Life Insurance. *I don't think so.*

Boys—Two. Pleasant Work. Salary. Apply 9–11am, Empire Building. *Doing what? Double nope.*

Experienced New and Used Car Salesmen. *Not a chance.*

He was about to close the paper when he saw:

40 Coal Loaders. Work every day. Pittsburgh seam. Good houses for family men. Paying $1.22 per car. *I could do that. But a whole coal car for $1.22? Crap! That's chump change!*

There was one more:

Wanted. Freight Car Sand Blasters. Standard Steel Car Company. Apply at the gate. *Railroad cars. That sounds good.*

John showed up to apply early the next morning. There was no interview—only an application to fill out.
I need a new name. The police are looking for John O'Brien.
Name: John Patrick Quinn
Age: 19
Address: Atlas Hotel, Pittsburgh

Experience: Sand blaster, New York Shipbuilding Corp.,
NY, NY

What are they gonna do? Call them?

Next of Kin: None

*Oh by the way, I'm a cold-blooded killer. I don't look like
one, do I.*

John handed his application to a clerk, and a few minutes
later, he had a job. "What? When can I start? Today?"

The foreman shook his hand and took him down to the
assembly area, pointing out the toilets and lockers.

After handing John a suit and goggles, he put him on
the line and gave him a pneumatic blasting gun that was
attached to a pressurized overhead pipe.

The foreman began: "Sounds like you know the drill
from shipyards. We don't like to put paint on a rusty car.
We're a little backed up. You're expected to do three cars a
day. Keep the pressure at medium or lower. Don't use more
sand than you have to. We're not a quarry. Hours are 7:30
to 5:30. Sharp. You have half an hour for lunch at 12:30.
A whistle will blow. Pay day is every Friday. No advances.
No drinking anywhere on the property. I'll be back later.
Any questions?"

"No, sir. Thank you, sir."

John had no idea what the foreman was talking about,
but he looked down the line and saw five or six men doing
the same thing. His station was on the end. The guy in the
nearest station tipped his helmet and nodded hello. John

faced his first car, then looked at the next guy to see what he did. *That looks easy,* he convinced himself.

After about an hour, John had one panel done. His neighbor had all four exterior sides finished and was about to begin working on the interior panels, the roof and the floor.

The whistle blew, and John left for lunch. Clearly this was going to be tougher than he thought. The other guy introduced himself as Lou, and suggested that John was standing too close with the nozzle, which covered less area.

"That's like trying to paint a house with a toothbrush," Lou explained.

John didn't bring a lunch, since he didn't realize he was going to be working today. Lou gave him an apple.

When they got back from lunch, John stood further back, and caught on pretty quickly. It was a good thing, because the foreman popped by around 3 pm, made a few observations, and seemed satisfied because he didn't say much.

John mastered the routine pretty quickly, and after a few weeks it was like he'd been doing this for years. Most of the men kept to themselves at break time, but Lou was helpful to talk with.

In mid-October 1929, the stock market began to fail, and orders slowed down. The backlog for steel cars was shrinking.

At the end of October, the market crashed and there was talk about layoffs.

By mid-December, all six sand blasters, along with most of the company, were out of a job.

Back to the newspaper:

Experienced Permanent Wavers Wanted. Male or Female. *A beautician?* John cleared his throat.

Experienced Corrugated Paper Box Salesman. *Nope.*

They're all shit jobs, but they want experienced shit job doers, he muttered to himself, reading about President Hoover before bed.

Before long, the Male Help Wanted ads dwindled to a trickle, and John began to think about other places. Maybe out west. Some kind of work less prone to layoffs. *But where and how?*

* * *

By the end of the year, John had blown through almost all the extra cash he had in his pocket when he left New York. Three cents for the Pittsburgh Gazette was starting to look like a luxury. One afternoon he ran into his old work pal, Lou, who was about to head west to Oregon where there was farm work. To get there, he would ride a train—for free.

It sounded too good to be true, but John got talked into it. Stuffing his clothes into a bag, along with a few groceries and sundries, they met up the next day at the park.

Lou explained the game plan. "We can't just go to Union Station and get on a train. That's for people. We need to go to the B&O Station, at Second and Smithfield, and catch a freight train. But we can't just jump on there either. The bulls will get you. There's a spot about a quarter mile away, where the trains are just beginning to speed up."

John nodded as though he understood what a bull was, and simply followed Lou's lead.

They walked on a dirt road that ran along the tracks, until they came upon a spot that looked good. They waited for 20 minutes until a locomotive appeared, followed by a train of about ten mostly empty boxcars. What luck.

As the train got closer, they started running, and five or six men unexpectedly leaped from behind the bushes and ran next to them.

Lou grabbed a door handle and jumped inside. Then he extended a hand to John, who almost slipped, but managed to pull himself up.

Moments later a young man, a boy really, appeared alongside the open door, running as fast as he could, with his hand outstretched. John reached for him. They made eye contact for a split second before the boy tripped over a railroad tie and landed face-first under one of the cars. A dull pop was the only sound John heard. The boy didn't have time to scream.

John was so stunned that he couldn't speak. He had never been around death—not even for his grandparents—until he shot his own boss. And now this. He couldn't get the kid's face out of his mind. Adrenalin and nausea coursed through his body for the next few hours.

As they approached a small station in northern Ohio, Lou stood in the doorway and motioned for John to get up.

"We can't wait around for the train to stop, or we're as good as dead. They'll catch you for sure. Bend your knees and roll when you hit the ground. Wait 'til those bushes up there. They'll break your fall."

John wasn't sure which was worse: leaping from a moving train or being caught when the train stopped. Lou yelled, "Now!" as he jumped.

John flew face-first into a shrub a few yards past Lou. He cut his lip, but nothing hurt. They dusted themselves off, and headed for the glow of a fire—a hobo camp, or jungle, where you could spend the night, buy a can of stew for a nickel, sit around a fire, and exchange stories.

Sometimes there were nearby farms where a sympathetic soul might give you a meal. A complex system of hobo hieroglyphics showed which houses had barking dogs, and which ones were inhabited by an owner with a gun, or by a kind lady who might feed them.

John and Lou didn't have to knock on any doors that first evening. They had brought enough to eat.

While most riders were simply laborers desperate for work, there were a lot more teenagers than John expected to see, coming from home circumstances far worse than anything he experienced in New Jersey.

John wondered about the kid who died earlier that day, and felt an overwhelming wave of guilt for not being able to pull him up in time, but he kept quiet.

John and Lou never really shared much about their personal histories. Lou looked like he was in his mid-30s, but he could have been younger. Always clean shaven at work, he looked pretty rough a few weeks later.

As they stared at the fire, Lou opened up a bit about having left his home in Philadelphia about a year earlier. He had a wife for a short time, but things didn't work out.

"I married a woman who hates me. That was my big mistake." He swigged a bit of whiskey from his flask and offered it to John, who quickly waved it off.

"All of your big mistakes are still in front of you, kid. What could you possibly be running away from?" Lou asked before he took another sip.

John shrugged as he thought about it. He almost told part of his story right there, but he quickly changed his mind. His home life really wasn't that bad compared to everyone else, and he couldn't discuss what happened in New York. He was a wanted man.

"How do you know she hated you?" John asked.

"It got to where she couldn't stand the way I chew, the way I walk and talk, the way I look, the way I laugh. She told me so."

"Then why did she marry you?"

"She got pregnant, but I'm not even sure it was mine."

John put his head on his bag and looked up at the stars, which he didn't remember ever seeing so clearly back in New Jersey or Pittsburgh.

The evening wore on, and everyone's confessionals gradually ran out of steam. John could feel the crushing weight of a hundred sad stories surrounding him. A big dog howled mournfully in the distance, as if to punctuate the somber scene.

While everyone snored and the fire faded to embers, John stayed awake all night—or so he thought—until he felt Lou shake his shoulder at about 5 am. It was still dark outside, but it was time to hit the rails again.

They repeated the same routine, although this time they found an open hopper car, which was used for grain, coal, or fertilizer.

Most riders managed to find boxcars. If a rider was lucky, he got a car filled with food, but that was quite rare. Some men lay on the steel frames under the cars, while others rode standing between the cars.

"Empty hopper cars are easy to hide in if they're empty, or if you can sit on top of a pile. But we definitely don't want to be in this thing when it gets filled with corn," Lou cautioned with a grin.

The hazards were many. Losing limbs was common. The two men heard stories about boxcar loads shifting while the train was moving, crushing the riders. Or doors that closed and locked, whether on purpose or on their own, and riders could die of thirst inside.

Lou's grin disappeared. "Then there's the bad guys. Sometimes it's the brakemen you have to look out for. They will move from car to car while you're rolling. They'll kick you off at the first stop. But the worst ones are the bulls. The bulls wait outside the stations. They're paid by the railroads to keep us off with clubs, guns and bare fists—whatever it takes to get you off the train. They'll even throw you off at full speed."

The reality of the ride began to sink in. Strangely, fear was never a problem for John back in New York. Maybe he was too naive to be scared, but he had carried a gun and his guys had his back. Lou continued as John listened carefully.

"Riding the freights is damn slow. If you get on the wrong train, they will make every…single…stop. A trip that takes a passenger train two days might take two weeks on several freight trains. That's why I carry some old employee timetables. They're outdated, but they're better than nothing."

By the time they got to Chicago, they looked and smelled ripe. They needed to find the Chicago & Northern tracks so they could continue on to Omaha. The men walked on industrial streets to avoid looking conspicuous in the business and residential areas.

More than once, a policeman threatened to lock them up unless they kept moving. Eventually they found the yard, and managed to grab hold of a ladder on a rolling train and stand between two cars that were leaving town. The Windy City receded behind them.

The men slid into a boxcar and were surprised to see it already occupied by two displaced families. There were locks on the next two cars, so they had to come back to the first car and cope with the sights, sounds, and smells of seven small children and their parents, living without running water or toilets.

John and Lou were stuck in that car for two long days as they rolled across Illinois and Iowa. They tried to stake out their territory by strategically placing their bags around them. They played cards to pass the time, but it was hard to avoid eye contact with the kids, who were eager to participate.

It didn't take long before the men realized that the kids didn't want to play cards. They were just hungry. They gave the kids what little food and candy they had, keeping a couple of stale rolls for themselves.

They were glad to get off the train after crossing the Missouri River in Omaha, where they changed to the Union Pacific railroad early the next morning. There was no time to buy food, because the stores weren't open yet.

As usual, they hid and waited outside the station, and stood up when the train they wanted was rolling. This train was moving pretty slowly, and they could catch it with merely a brisk walk. John took the lead this time, and Lou was right behind him.

John grabbed the door frame of a steel boxcar and climbed in. As he turned around to pull Lou in, a bull came out of nowhere, running alongside the train. The man jumped up and tore at Lou's shirt, which popped all the buttons off. Then he cracked a wooden bat squarely onto Lou's cap.

John pulled Lou in, and the bull started to climb into the car right behind him. The bull's face was angry, red and sweaty, and he was reaching his arm out, trying to find something to hold on to. He finally got a grip on a side ladder and swung around to get inside the door, dropping his bat in the process. John and Lou both kicked at the man's hands until he let go and tumbled along the tracks.

"You OK, Lou?"

"Yeah I think so." Lou pulled his hat up and touched the back of his head. There was blood on his fingers, but it didn't look too bad. The cap must have cushioned the blow. It was a close call.

There wasn't much to see out on the plains. They watched the telephone wires curve up, then down, from pole to pole, mile after mile. They played cards and laughed when Lou pointed to a small metal plate saying they were riding in a car manufactured by the Standard Steel Car Company of Pittsburgh PA.

"Hah! Nothing but the finest in accommodations."

At dusk, as the train rolled across the cold plains of Nebraska, Lou complained that he was seeing double. The sunset was now a fading thin strip of red along the flat horizon. John began to worry, like maybe he was in over his head. Taking care of himself was tough enough, but an injured buddy who couldn't see straight?

"You'll be better tomorrow," he tried to reassure Lou.

John lay back and tried to sleep, but he could hear Lou moaning quietly, "I should never have left. I'm sorry I left. I shouldn't have left. I'll do anything."

"Shhh. Try to get some sleep, Lou." John gave him his jacket.

After a long chilly night, the sky became dark grey, and John could see Lou sleeping soundly. It would soon be time to jump off, but when Lou opened his eyes, he stared blankly.

"I can't see. I can't see a damn thing." Both men felt panic as the train slowed down. There would be no way for Lou to jump. "I can't see! Dammit!"

John couldn't leave Lou here, but he couldn't call for help either. He decided to wait until they were in a larger town, when he could pull Lou off the train and hope that someone would help him—assuming they didn't get caught before then.

John created a space behind some stacked pallets and dragged Lou by the armpits toward the hidden shelter. This would have to do until they got to a large town. Lou had always been the navigator, but the timetables were in the pocket of the shirt that he lost. Now John had no idea which train they were on, or where it would stop.

They rode through the empty flatness, with frequent stops in the middle of nowhere. A grain silo, a warehouse, and a couple of trucks were apparently sufficient to give a place a station name, even without a real town nearby. It took forever.

John knew he had to do something soon, but sleep overtook him. He was deep in the middle of a dream when he felt the train lurch forward sharply. He ran to the door to see where they were, just as a sign saying "Cheyenne WY" slid past. But they weren't slowing down; they were accelerating. John had slept through the stop, and it was already early dawn.

"Dammit!"

He nudged Lou, but there was no response. John's heart began to pound.

"Come on, buddy. We're almost there." He shook him harder, but Lou's head swung to one side. He wasn't breathing, and his lips were blue.

John stared at his face and sobbed for the first time since he was a child—for Lou, for the guilt of sleeping through Cheyenne, for not saving that kid who was trying to jump onto the train, for killing Patrick Duffy, and for the cold reality of where he now was.

He sat in the doorway with his knees to his chest, shaking, and waited for the train to pull into the first town that appeared, no matter how small.

November 1929, La Salle, CO

John pulled his jacket off the body. It was still warm. There was a pencil in Lou's bag, so he wrote Lou's name on a scrap of paper, adding "Philadelphia PA." He tucked the paper partially under Lou's belt, grabbed his nearly empty water canteen, and jumped off into some tumbleweeds just before the train rolled into the rail yard of La Salle, Colorado, at the western edge of the Great Plains.

It was freezing just before the sun came up. John walked next to the tracks toward the station, waiting for the handful of trucks to leave after unloading their cargo onto the train.

US Highway 85 ran parallel to the tracks, about 50 yards away. It was too early for cars. A road sign said Greeley was 6 miles to the right, and Denver was 48 miles to the left. It was dead quiet, and John stood for a moment in the spotlight of the rail yard, wishing he had a heavier jacket. His stomach growled angrily.

Most of the small town appeared to be on the other side of the highway, and he meandered slowly in that direction.

His nerves were on edge as house lights came on and people prepared for their day. The sky looked heavy, and fog was coming out of his mouth as his shoes crunched on top of the gravel and fallen leaves along the side of the road. It was impossible to walk without making noise.

A hot shower sounded good, and the smell of sizzling bacon drifted down the street. John could see a man drinking coffee in his kitchen, and he thought of the automat in New York. *Shower, coffee and bacon. Shower, coffee and bacon.*

For the first time in his life, John realized that he didn't have a friend or an acquaintance within at least a thousand miles— or maybe two thousand miles. Not a soul on the planet knew him as John Quinn. He was truly on his own again. It's what he had wanted, but it didn't sound so appealing this morning.

A middle-aged man sat in his car as it warmed up, looking in the rearview mirror when he noticed John moving in the shadows. It was time to get off the street.

Along the left side of the road was a dark house with a stable in the back, which he approached carefully. There weren't any horses inside, and from the network of cobwebs across his path, the building seemed to have been unused for some time. A rusty hand pump stood outside, and the water tasted like mud, but it was better than nothing. A pile of hay looked welcoming in the corner and he lay down, exhausted. A rat ran across a rafter and stared at the intruder.

After napping for a few hours, he left his bag in the stable and went looking for whatever would pass for a downtown. If he didn't find some food, he would starve.

For a small sleepy farm village, John was surprised that it held a pharmacy, a general store, a grocery store, a barber shop, a lumber yard—and a pool hall. A jolt of excitement perked his spirits. He had a quarter and a nickel left over from his journey.

His dilemma was whether to buy food at the grocery and try to make it last for one or two days, or to risk everything to win a few rounds of pool.

The pool hall looked empty and foreboding from outside, and he wasn't feeling lucky enough to gamble his last 30¢, so he opted for the grocery.

Surely he could make a few slices of ham, some cheese, a box of crackers and a couple of cans of beans last for two or three days. If only there was a place to cook bacon and make coffee.

There was a park next door, along with a picnic table. Reaching into his sack of food, he ate greedily, making himself slow down before the food disappeared.

At the end of the afternoon, he walked back toward the stable.

Maybe I should hop another freight tomorrow.

The clouds opened up for a few minutes as the sun was setting, and he got a glimpse of the distant Rockies for the first time. He'd never seen a mountain with his own eyes before, let alone an entire jagged range. Turning to the west, he stood still while his mouth opened unconsciously. The sun's rays were radiating like a deity from behind a purple peak. It didn't look real, but it spoke to him as if God himself was doing the magic.

The transition from day to night came quickly, and he found himself next to the stable again, listening for voices before walking in.

The wind began to howl outside, and it felt good to sit on the soft straw. He had returned just in time. If only there was a fire for warming himself and a can of beans. He was tired of being cold and eating cold food.

Holy crap. I don't have a damn can opener! What was I thinking?

In the corner was a small workbench with a few tools hanging on an adjacent wall. He pulled down a hammer and chisel and tapped a ring of holes on top of the can. It made some noise, but he worked quickly and pried the lid off.

John returned to his pile of hay to eat from the can, being careful not to cut his lips on the jagged tin.

Bare branches brushed against the wooden siding of the stable, and the sounds didn't seem out of place until he realized that they were actually shuffling footsteps, and they were getting louder.

A sneeze almost escaped as he held his breath. *Shit!* The door opened and a figure appeared, holding a shotgun and a lantern. John jumped up and hid behind a post before he could make out who it was.

An older woman's voice called out, "I know you're in here. Step out where I can see you, or I'll shoot."

John could outrun a woman, he was sure of it, but maybe not one with a gun. He was cornered, and there was no back door. He stepped out from behind the post and lifted his hands.

In front of him was a plump-faced woman in her mid-60s. She lifted the lantern, which reflected off her spectacles and made it difficult to see her eyes.

"What are you doing in my barn?"

John looked down. "I'm sorry, ma'am."

"Well? Who are you?" She raised her gun higher as she calculated how she might hold him at gunpoint while sliding into the house to call the sheriff.

"I'm John Quinn, ma'am. I just got here, and I had no place to stay. It looked empty."

"What are you doing here?

"Just trying to get some sleep."

"No. What are you doing in La Salle?"

"I'm looking for work, ma'am." John explained that he was laid off in Pittsburgh, and how he and his pal Lou had caught a series of freight trains and headed west, until Lou was killed by a railroad guard.

"What about your family?"

He still had a New York accent—there was no covering that up. He told her he was born to two Irish immigrants who died before he was ten. He had no family.

As she listened, she lowered her gun and her demeanor softened.

"Well, you should give thanks for your life," she said.

The woman walked over and told him to get on his knees. Before he could ask why, she knelt and pulled him down by the hand.

Her tone became somber. "Let us pray. Dear Lord Jesus, I know I am a sinner. I believe You died for my sins. Right now, I turn from my sins and open the door of my heart and life. I confess You as my personal Lord and Savior."

Afterwards, she looked at him and asked, "Aren't you gonna say Amen?"

John had never been inside a church, and he had certainly never uttered a Christian prayer in his life.

"Amen?" he said, as though he was asking a question.

"You must be hungry. Come inside."

John couldn't believe his good fortune, but he also wondered what new predicament he had gotten himself into.

He washed his hands and face, and joined her for his first home-cooked meal since he left New Jersey.

Bessie Thompson was a 63-year-old widow who was trying to keep her property going. Her husband, a minister, had passed away the year before. She was hungry for someone to talk to, and talk she did, including prayers for everything.

She brought him some blankets, and he slept in the stable.

In the morning she invited him into her bright yellow kitchen for breakfast. The house was warm, and there was bacon and coffee, which he now drank black. The low sun shone through the windowpanes and into their eyes, but John asked if she could please keep the curtains open.

As he took his first sip from the cup, John heard what sounded like a low rumble of distant thunder, but the sky was clear. The sound repeated itself every few minutes. He made a comment to Bessie, who laughed and told him about the "beet dumps" at the train station. Sugar beets were the largest crop in the area, and large trucks would pull up to empty train cars, dump their contents into the metal cars, and make room for the next truck. This was the tail end of the season, but the racket began every October.

Bessie let him stay there for two weeks, and John did some chores around the house. He knew nothing about repairing fences or fixing furniture, but Mrs. Thompson knew even less. He asked for help more than once at the hardware store a few blocks away.

When it came to cleaning a chicken coop, there wasn't a lot to know. It was a smelly job, and the chickens were grouchy, but he wasn't in a position to complain. The eggs tasted great, and on Sunday he watched her kill a rooster and prepare it for supper. She knew he was from the big city, and she clearly enjoyed showing him how these things were done in rural Colorado, even if his eyes were closed for much of the time.

The following Sunday it was his turn, and she watched closely as John shut his eyes once again and did the deed. He felt disgust, guilt and relief, but said nothing. He had seen more than enough violent death during the past year, and killing a chicken evoked a visceral reaction that surprised him. He'd be happy for the rest of his life to disassociate his supper from the animal that it once was.

That evening, Mrs. Thompson told him about a friend of her late husband who needed some help. He lived forty miles northwest of La Salle, outside the farming community of Wellington, on the other side of Fort Collins. It was the last town before Wyoming.

The man was George Conway, who had nine children, plus three who died young. He had recently lost an arm in a farming accident. His boys, except for the oldest one, were still too young to handle a medium-sized sugar beet farm and the gaggle of sheep and chickens that helped to pay the bills. He needed help, but couldn't pay much, if anything. But it was free room and board, and it was a chance to learn about farming.

Bessie drove John into Fort Collins, and he hugged her goodbye. "You saved my life, Bessie. I won't forget you."

George Conway pulled up a few minutes later in a 1925 model T Runabout pickup, and looked John up and down before saying anything. "Well aren't you a short one," he snarked.

John stood at 5'8" and 140 lbs. *I'm not that little.* George's comment still stung.

George got out and said, "You drive."

"I don't know how to drive sir. I grew up in New York. Hardly anyone drives there. Except drivers."

"Well you're 20. It's time you learned. Get in. I'll tell you how."

George seemed a bit impatient, but showed him all the knobs, levers and pedals while the car sat idling next to the curb. John recited what he'd been told: "Okay, the middle pedal is R for Reverse. Don't accidentally touch that while I'm driving. The left pedal is the clutch. Press it for low gear, and then release it while pushing the hand lever forward for high gear, which is also a brake for parking the car. The third pedal is the transmission brake, which is for slowing down, but don't forget to throttle back at the same time. The throttle lever is on the steering wheel, not on the floor. And don't forget to adjust the spark advance or she'll stall. Is that right, Mr. Conway?"

"Yep. Let's go," George said as they pulled away from the curb. "Don't ride the clutch, dammit!" he hollered more than once, as John drove through stop signs, sideswiped other cars, startled horses, and stalled the engine every few minutes.

Soon they left Fort Collins behind, and the main concern became avoiding the countless mailboxes that were perched so unreasonably close to the road. At one point, it looked like George was going to jump out of the car, but John started whistling a made-up tune, and that seemed to calm things down a bit.

John couldn't imagine how George could possibly manage to steer the car, work the throttle, push the high gear lever, and press everything else with one arm. This was clearly a two-arm operation, but he never saw George drive again after that first day.

After driving several miles north, mostly in a straight line, they pulled up to a white farm house. George reached over to turn off the engine, and the car backfired to announce their arrival.

John got out with his bag, and started to walk toward the porch. George shook his head no, pointing to the back of the house. "That room behind the garage is yours. And that outhouse too. Breakfast is at 6. We'll bring your lunch and supper. We'll talk about what needs to be done in the morning."

Although there was never a formal introduction, it didn't take too long to figure out that there were four daughters, ages 6, 12, 16 and 20, and five sons, ages 1, 4, 5, 9 and 19.

Two children died years ago, and one died only several weeks earlier. Josephine Conway, who had given birth to 12 children over a 22 year period, was still despondent over the death of a third child. The girls were taking up the slack in household duties when they weren't in school.

The oldest boy, Carl, was the only kid with enough muscle to help out with labor-intensive farm duties. He was easily distracted and nowhere to be seen when it was time to lift something heavy, but always around when there was ball game in the front yard.

John quickly learned how to be a farm hand, and ran errands in old man Conway's pickup.

That first winter was slow, and when the spring of 1930 arrived, it was time to prepare for the annual sugar beet crop, which is where nearly all of the family income came from.

Mrs. Conway stayed in her room most of the time, and her meals were brought upstairs to her. John got to know the kids a bit, and they asked a lot of questions about New York. But if George overheard any of it, he quickly changed the subject. There was no reason for any of the kids to get ideas about moving off to the big city.

George had settled in the area around 1905, had a few crop failures, and then tried his hand at farming up in Wyoming. After running into a water rights dispute, he returned to Wellington several years later. Things were finally picking up financially.

On Sundays, the family went to a Baptist church, including Mrs. Conway. John stayed behind, making the excuse that he was Catholic, which made George wince each time he heard it mentioned.

George knew all about Catholics. They weren't real Christians. They spoke in Latin, spent a lot of money on churches, and they had a pope who wore red slippers for cryin' out loud.

1930 was a great year for sugar beets, and John made $600, enough for an occasional weekend drive into Fort Collins for a movie. His life was becoming stable and predictable for the first time in years.

Colorado was one of the last states to require a license to drive, and in the fall of 1930, John went into town to fill out the application. When he returned home, he carried a card bearing the name of John Patrick Quinn on it, with a birth date of October 1909. His name and age were now official. He couldn't quit staring at the piece of paper.

Northeastern Colorado had its share of eastern European immigrants, attracted by the sugar beet work. There was some anti-immigration sentiment due to the scarcity of jobs, and as a result, those communities mostly kept to themselves.

One afternoon, John took George into town to buy some supplies. In a hardware store, he felt someone tap on his shoulder. He turned around.

"Isadore! Isadore Katz! What are you doing here?"

Hearing his former name was a jolt. "Excuse me?"

"You don't remember me? Benjamin. From Jersey City! From the synagogue! How is your family? I can't believe it!"

John was mortified, but he hardened his face and said, "You have me mixed up with someone else. I'm John Quinn. I'm from New York, not New Jersey. And I'm not a Jew."

"But…"

John looked over at George, who had a vague look of disgust on his face.

George didn't have a reason to hate Jews. He had never met one…that he knew of. Once in a while he complained, like most people he knew, that he was "Jewed" out of money by someone, but it wasn't personal. One thing he couldn't tolerate, however, was a liar. And now he wondered whether his farm hand was really named Isadore Katz.

George squinted his eyes and looked squarely at John. His mind buzzed with questions. *What other secrets does he have? Who names their kid Isadore?*

Benjamin persisted. "But your sister Jean! Remember we were engaged?"

"Listen, you're mistaken, mister," John said to Benjamin as he turned around and walked to the cashier.

John and George left the store and walked to the truck. John knew he had just survived a close call, but he didn't want to raise more doubts by bringing it up. He pointed to some dark rain clouds forming to the west.

George sat quietly in the passenger seat, and considered what difference it would make if John actually was lying about his identity.

He does good work, and he otherwise seems honest. But why would he change his name? What or who is he running from?

They didn't discuss the encounter on the way home, and it never came up again, but it haunted John for a long time. Once in a while when George gave him a certain look, John felt like George knew the truth, and would use it against him one day.

In reality, though, George gradually forgot about the incident. He had bigger things to worry about.

Very little rain fell in 1931, and the crops fared poorly. They were able to augment with more irrigation, but the fall harvest was about half that of previous years. John drove the truck back and forth to the beet dumps, but money was becoming scarce, and the Conways were showing signs of financial stress.

The girls wore dresses that Mrs. Conway made from the fabric of feed and flour sacks, which came printed with floral designs on them. More than once, John could hear their tearful protests about being seen in a feed sack dress, but soon it became clear that most of their classmates were in the same situation.

The oldest son, Carl, escaped the farm by getting married and moving far away to New Jersey, of all places.

1932, Fort Collins, CO

By the time the summer of 1932 came, it was clear that Colorado was in midst of a serious drought. They didn't realize it at the time, but this was the beginning of a ten year dry spell. The Dust Bowl was developing to the south, forcing the migration of thousands of farmers and workers to the west coast.

George talked often about selling the farm and moving to Fort Collins. The girls were upset, especially the 15 year old, Laverne, who had a lot of school friends in the area.

John lived in the room behind the garage, so he couldn't hear everything, but now and then the back screen door would slam, and he'd see Laverne sitting and crying on the steps. Initially she covered her face out of embarrassment, and he would try to avoid eye contact. After it became a regular occurrence, it was almost like she hoped he would notice.

He started to spend more time in Fort Collins while running errands for old man Conway. He began looking for other work opportunities while he had the luxury of time.

One afternoon, Laverne asked if she could get a lift into town. John wasn't sure if her father would approve, but she said he wouldn't care.

On the 20-minute ride down, Laverne sat a little closer than a typical passenger would. She slapped his knee when she wanted to emphasize a point, and she gave him her undivided attention whenever he spoke.

John believed that she was flirting, although it could have been his hormones hallucinating. Besides, she was only 15 and he was 22. Well, he was actually only 18, he rationalized, but she was still too young.

Growing up in a family with so many siblings was a horrible fate, she complained. So was having a tired mother and a father who worked too many hours. She couldn't wait to get out of the house. "The day I turn 18, I'm gone," she swore, as she snapped her fingers.

John grinned as he listened, sympathizing with more of her story than he could let on.

"What about your family?" she asked, and was surprised to hear that he not only didn't have parents or siblings, but no aunts, uncles or cousins.

"Wow. I'm really jealous," she said. "I'm so tired of my family. I don't hate them, but I can't ever get a moment to myself. Sometimes I think I'm going crazy."

Laverne stared at John for a full minute as he drove, and he could see her looking at him from the corner of his eye. He smelled the faint scent of her bath soap, and could feel her breath in his ear as she spoke. She had developed womanly curves while he was busy working, and the summer sun had brought out a sprinkling of freckles that he never noticed before.

John caught himself and struggled to change the subject. "Sounds like your dad is going sell the farm. I'm going to look for work in Fort Collins."

She pouted and looked rather cute when she did.

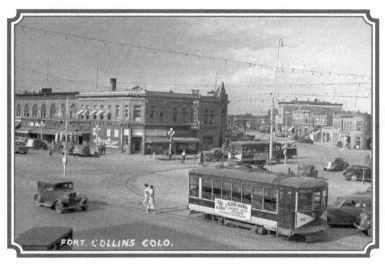

Fort Collins, 1937
Fort Collins Museum of Discovery H02746

They pulled into a diagonal parking spot, and John came around the car and opened the door for her. They agreed to meet in an hour for the trip home. Without any warning or hesitation, she leaned in and kissed his cheek. "Thanks for the lift, John."

Later that week, John landed a job driving a truck for the Fort Collins Dairy. He thanked the Conways, got his suitcase packed, and asked for a lift into town. Everyone came onto the porch to wave goodbye, but Laverne hung back in the front door frame. John looked right at her, and her eyes were red. She turned around and walked back into the house before the car started to move.

The job was monotonous and involved hours of sitting, punctuated with backbreaking work, but it was a steady paycheck.

Not too long afterwards, George Conway sold the farm, and the entire family moved into a tiny house in downtown Fort Collins. John managed to repay a favor to George when he helped him to get a job working for the same dairy.

1933 and 1934 came and went, and the Great Drought and Great Depression took their toll on the region, from Northeast Colorado down to Texas. Times were tough for practically everyone.

John met and dated a few girls from work, but felt like he had nothing to offer them. Women at the dairy were looking for established men with financial stability, much the way eighth grade girls back in New Jersey preferred older boys.

It was a lonely time.

In the fall of 1934, the dairy had a company picnic at Fort Collins Park for Labor Day. There was live music, and everyone brought their families. It was unseasonably warm, and people spread their blankets and baskets along the shore of the pond. John decided to go at the last minute, and picked a quiet spot on the lawn. He was eating his lunch and listening to a group of fiddle players when he saw a familiar face walking toward him.

"Hello, stranger," Laverne said. "Did you miss me?"

John looked up at her, and couldn't believe it had been two years since he last saw her. She was going to be 17 in a couple of weeks, although she looked even more grown up today.

They sat on his picnic blanket and talked about her school and his work. The house her folks had bought was tiny, and she had to share a room with two of her sisters. She was miserable, but school activities kept her busy and out of the house as much as possible.

Before she left, she gave John her phone number. This time, she leaned in to kiss him on the lips, then gave him a wistful smile over her shoulder as she walked away.

Before long they were dating, initially on the sly. She would tell her mom she was going to a movie with her friends, and meet John instead. They went to movies, ate in restaurants and walked in the park.

Coming from large families, they had a lot in common, even though John was the only one who appreciated it most of the time.

John worried about George finding out, but by the time 1935 arrived, he had decided to marry Laverne, and he realized he was going to need to deal with George eventually.

When spring arrived, it was becoming too difficult to sneak around, and their relationship was out in the open after Mrs. Conway saw them kissing on a sidewalk in town.

It wasn't clear if he was imagining it or not, but George seemed to avoid John at work.

Is it because old man Conway's 17-year-old daughter is dating a 25-year-old (even though I'm really only 21)? Is the idea of me being Catholic too much for him, or is it the suspicion that I'm actually a Jewish kid from New Jersey—an imposter named Isadore?

Laverne knew her father wouldn't approve of marriage until she was 18 anyway. Her older sister eloped at age 17, and it did not sit well with George at all. John and Laverne would have to wait nine months, and even then, there was the question of whether to ask permission or just get married like two grownups.

The couple pondered the decision over the summer and by August, John had worked up the nerve to ask George for Laverne's hand, even though she'd soon be an adult anyway.

When the afternoon came, John came over for Sunday dinner. He had rehearsed his speech, and was ready to discuss Catholicism, his work prospects, the ideal family size and anything else old man Conway might throw at him. If being Jewish came up, he would just deny it again.

Walking into the house, the smell of frying liver assaulted his nose. Not a great start. He almost gagged from the smell as he shook George's left hand.

There were still a lot of kids living at home, but the house was a small fraction of the size of their old farm house in Wellington. The meal was uneventful, and there were lots of onions and ketchup, thank God.

While the lack of elbow room reminded John of his family dinners in Jersey City, hardly anyone spoke during this particular meal. They were much quieter than when they lived on the farm, which made John nervous. They probably knew why he was there, but he couldn't figure out how it was going to go. He could hear the clanging of silverware on plates, the sound of water being swallowed and of food being chewed. John missed his big, talkative family at that moment.

After dinner, the two men stepped out onto the front porch.

John stammered and cleared his throat, but George put his hand on John's shoulder and said, "John, just take her. There's too many mouths to feed, and she's getting to be quite a handful. I love her, but I've done all I can do for her. She's all yours now."

That's it? Really? What a relief.

Two weeks later Laverne turned 18, and two days later John and Laverne were married by a justice of the peace.

Her parents were there, her siblings, and several school friends. John had no one. He wished for a moment that he could call his parents and give them the good news, but he knew that they wouldn't approve of him marrying a girl who wasn't Jewish.

John managed to save up for a honeymoon splurge at the glass-domed Northern Hotel in Fort Collins for $7.50, where each room came with a free miniature bar of soap.

Afterwards, the couple made their home in a tiny house on a rural route near Timnath, about ten miles east of Fort Collins.

John didn't want anything more to do with sugar beets, so he found a job as a farm hand working with dairy cows.

The Quinns were just far enough away from Laverne's family to not have to eat there every night, far enough that her family couldn't drop by unannounced while the young couple were lounging around in their pajamas, but close enough to visit for the holidays. That suited John and Laverne just fine.

After a couple of weeks in the house, Laverne teased John.

"I'll bet you were a cute baby. Don't you have any baby pictures?"

"No. I got nothing from my parents," he replied.

"Don't you have a photo of them? Who do you look like more?"

"I almost don't remember. I was told I look like both of them."

"Where in Ireland were they from?"

"County Cork," the only county name he could think of.

"And their names were John and Mary? Didn't you have any other family?"

"No. I was an only child, and I'd rather not talk about it."

"I'm sorry, dear. It must have been terrible being all alone in the world. I'll bet you still have relatives in Ireland."

John looked at his shoes.

"Maybe we can go one day. John? Hello?"

Every St Patrick's Day beginning in 1936, she made corned beef and cabbage for John, hoping to make up for his lost Irish heritage.

* * *

Back in Jersey City, Willie was the last of Isadore's brothers to get married. The bedroom was finally empty of boys. Eight years after Isadore left, Sam and Minnie finally stripped Isadore's bed and sold the furniture. The room became a catch-all for boxes and sewing materials. Once in a while, Isadore's name would come up briefly at the dinner table, and it was always accompanied by a wistful sigh.

* * *

In 1937 John and Laverne had their first child, a little girl who was named after John's "mother," Mary. At first glance, she looked more like her mother than her father, but when the light hit her eyes just right, John could see Minnie's face very clearly.

From John's perspective, there were plenty of Katz kids sitting around the dinner table back in Jersey City, before and after he left. He convinced himself long ago that his absence would make no difference to anyone, but now there was a new baby who would never know John's parents. One day he would have to tell his daughter that Grandpa John and Grandma Mary were dead, knowing full well that she was being robbed of her real grandparents, Sam and Minnie, and that she was being stolen from them. His decision to leave home years ago was now affecting innocent bystanders.

One morning, John began writing to his parents to let them know he was a father. He held a fountain pen in his hand, and stared at the blank sheet of paper on the little table in the corner of the kitchen.

Hi Mom and Dad—it's Isadore, but my name is John now.

He scrunched his eyes in thought. His pen didn't move.

No. That's not it. Why would I be writing now, after nearly ten years? They think I hate them, but I don't. I never did. I was a punk kid who didn't know any better. For their sake, I hope they don't miss me.

He continued. *I'm the father of a beautiful little girl. She looks like my wife Laverne, but her eyes look just like mom's.*

He paused again to gather his thoughts. *Why am I doing this now? To rub salt in their wounds?*

His pen moved again. *I hope she grows up to be a somebody in spite of her father. And I hope she never breaks my heart the way I've broken yours.*

Then he scribbled angrily all over the paper, wadded it up and threw it in the trash.

"I just can't," he said aloud. *It's too late.*

"Did you say something, honey?" Laverne called from the other room.

John knew he couldn't have done better than to marry a farm girl. Every year Laverne put up fruits and vegetables in jars destined for the winter basement, and she was just as comfortable swinging an axe to chop wood. John was less of a city boy than when he first got to Colorado, but he was still no match for Laverne's frontier know-how. He respected her for it.

The Quinns lived in their little house for three more years, making friends with their neighbors, playing with Mary and puttering in the garden. Saturday nights were for pinochle, and they switched houses every week. A new radio brought them their favorite shows every evening, including FDR's fireside chats.

These good years ended when the drought finally caught up with the dairy industry in 1940, and the Fort Collins Dairy went out of business—just before the rains resumed.

It was time for a change of address.

1940–1942, Cripple Creek, CO

Laverne kept in touch with her old high school friend, Ruby, who had recently moved to a gold mining town called Cripple Creek, at the edge of the Rocky Mountains, down near Pike's Peak. Her husband Ray was a contractor at a gold mine where production was booming, and he had a small crew working for him. He was making good money, and Laverne made sure to mention this to John whenever a new letter came.

What John didn't know was that Laverne was pregnant again. She knew first-hand what a struggle it was for her father to feed the family, but at least they lived on a farm. John and Laverne had nothing, and she was terrified.

One day Laverne jumped up from the kitchen table to deal with Mary, and John noticed a half-finished letter to Ruby. Laverne's coffee cup covered the top portion of the letter, while a pencil and napkin obscured the bottom, but this much was visible:

"...don't know how we're going to make it. John would never ask, he's too proud, but if you think that Ray is doing well

enough that maybe he could use more help, perhaps he could ask us if we know of anyone interested in moving down…"

Laverne returned and quickly scooped up her dishes along with the letter, not realizing that John had already snuck a peak at it.

He was embarrassed to have his wife looking for a job for him, but nothing was panning out in Timnath or Fort Collins, so he kept quiet about the letter. A week later, Laverne got a response from Ruby, parts of which she read out loud:

"Ray's working long hours because help is so hard to find down here. I worry about him not getting enough sleep… He's thinking of running a Help Wanted ad in Fort Collins, but if you two know of anyone…"

"Dear, maybe things would be better down there. What do you think?" Laverne asked.

John shrugged his shoulders and pretended that he didn't know about the letter. It didn't really matter at this point anyway. His pride wasn't worth starving over. He thought he should feel humiliated by what she had done, but strangely he didn't. Instead, he was proud of her.

John and Laverne packed up their old car and drove 165 miles down to Cripple Creek, sight unseen. They found a tiny place to rent on Bennett Street, almost at the edge of the city limits.

The main part of the town was a few blocks long, lined with brick buildings and wooden plank sidewalks. It looked like a set from a wild west movie.

After being in Colorado for almost six years, John finally felt like he was living in the Rockies rather than the Great Plains. Visually, it was a huge change from Timnath.

The Quinns went to Ruby and Ray's house for dinner, and they hit it off. The following Monday, John started working for Ray in the Elkton Gold mine just outside of town.

Cripple Creek, around 1940
Courtesy of the Linda Irene Tingvik Collection

At 9,500 feet in elevation, it was easy to get winded, but every morning John would walk a half a mile into town, and Ray would give him a lift up the hill to the mine. The work was grueling and dangerous. Fatalities occurred almost daily, but the money was good in 1940 and John wasn't in a position to complain. He was glad to be finished with being a farm hand and driving a truck.

Ray reminded John a bit of himself. He was short and thin, and roughly the same age. His ears stuck out, and he didn't care what the world thought of him. He was in charge of his own destiny, and nobody gave him anything. His contracting operation was large enough that he had a business office in the center of Cripple Creek. John admired his drive and his business smarts.

Gold mine at Cripple Creek
Courtesy of the Linda Irene Tingvik Collection

Meanwhile, Laverne's sister Ruth, who was 18, moved down from Fort Collins with her new husband, who was lured by an accounting job in a gold bullion office.

Ruth was also expecting a child, and she spent a lot of time with Laverne and Ruby while Ray and John toiled with pick axes and mallets during their long days underground.

The first winter was bitterly cold, but the snow was light. John marveled at the deep blue crystalline skies of the high altitude Rockies, and the way the stars looked close enough to touch at night. Pine trees scented the air most of the time, except when the winds drifted over the mines and filled the town with the smell of rotten eggs from the sulfur that accompanied the gold deposits.

For the first time since leaving New York, John had enough money in his pocket to not have to worry about making ends meet. It was almost too good to be true.

The spring of 1941 meant that Laverne and Ruth were due to have their babies. There was a phone in the foreman's office, and he was to be called if either woman went into labor.

In March, Laverne gave birth to a son, and they named him John, after John's Irish "father," John. They had a good laugh when they thought about adding a dynastic "III" after his name on the birth certificate, but it sounded too pompous, so they opted for plain old "John Quinn."

In April, Ruth went into labor a couple of weeks early, and the hospital called her husband to come as quickly as possible.

John caught a lift back home at the end of his shift, and found a note from Laverne on the kitchen table. There was a complication with Ruth's delivery, and she had gone to the hospital to help her sister.

He walked in the direction of the hospital, and halfway there, he recognized Laverne, Mary and a stroller slowly moving in the dark. Laverne was wailing, and three year old Mary was trying to comfort her.

Laverne collapsed into John's arms as she approached.

The baby was stillborn, and then Ruth bled to death during the delivery. She was only 19, married for nine short months, and now she was gone.

Laverne fell into shock over her sister's untimely death, and then into a full-blown depression.

Ruby helped look after Laverne and the kids while the men were were at work. John felt ill-equipped to help Laverne cope with the loss of her sister, while taking care of the kids and working full-time. He began to confide in Ray, especially when they stopped by the saloon for a whiskey and a weekly game of pool after work.

The two families did things together over the summer. In the fall, the aspens all around the town turned a brilliant yellow, which was poetically appropriate for a gold mining town.

The winter of 1941 began with news about the Japanese attack on Pearl Harbor and the declaration of war. Then the heaviest snowfall in 30 years landed on Cripple Creek. Some days it wasn't possible to walk into town, let alone to get to the mines.

They all spent Christmas and New Year's Eve together and made the best of it. Card games for the grown-ups and Christmas for the kids. Just after New Year's Day, the roads were clear enough to walk the streets, and the two men trudged into town to have a drink.

As they sat on their bar stools, John noticed a middle-aged guy at the other end of the bar, looking at him from across the smoky room. The man wasn't familiar, but his interest was obvious. He seemed to be trying to figure out where he knew John from. When he started to get up and come over, John turned to Ray and said, "Let's go."

"Why? C'mon—let's have another," Ray said.

"No. Let's go now. Now."

Ray gave John a quizzical look and hesitated, but John pulled on his sleeve and they quickly headed for the front door.

"What the hell was that all about?"

"Nothing. Forget it," John replied.

"No, really. What happened back there?" Ray asked.

"It's a long story. Some other time."

"It's Friday night. Come over to the house and we'll have another drink. Ruby and the kids are asleep by now."

They sat at Ray's kitchen table and talked quietly.

John had carried his secrets around for nearly 15 years now. They were getting heavier rather than lighter with each passing year, and the guilt of shooting Pat Duffy continued to haunt him. He was tired of worrying about being recognized.

Nobody knew about his past—not even his own wife. But he had too much to drink, and now he felt an overwhelming urge to tell his story to someone he trusted.

"You have to swear not to tell a soul. Not even Laverne or Ruby."

"Scout's honor," Ray said as he crossed his heart. "Hope to die," he said, mixing his expressions. "You can skip the needle in my eye."

The men laughed before John abruptly changed the tone with, "I killed a man." Then he told Ray the whole story from the beginning.

There was so much to explain that he scarcely stopped to take a breath. When he was finished, Ray just sat there as though he was sleeping with his eyes open. John nudged him.

"Did I put you to sleep?"

"That's some story," Ray said, as if in a trance. Neither man said anything for a full minute, until John wondered if he'd made a mistake, or if Ray just had too much to drink.

John stood up to leave. "Well, thanks for listening."

Ray nodded his head once, without blinking. "Thanks for telling me."

After he let himself out, John glanced through the window and could see Ray sitting in the same position, staring at a candle with no expression on his face.

His first instinct was to worry about whatever Ray was thinking, but that was outweighed by a tremendous sense of relief and gratitude that he had at last found a friend he could confide in.

They didn't speak over the weekend, and Monday morning he and Ray rode in the pickup truck up to the mine. Ray seemed normal enough, if subdued, during the brief ride.

"You OK?" John asked.

"Yeah I'm OK. I just have a lot on my mind," Ray said.

"Did I spill too many beans?"

"No, not at all."

Ray stopped the truck in the middle of the dirt road, and turned to face John.

"Listen, I killed a man too, and I'm not proud of it. And it wasn't an accident, but I'd do it again all the same. I had to make peace with myself long ago. We can talk about it after work, if you've got time for a beer."

Ray smirked. "Then we'll both have some dirt on each other."

"You bet. I'd like that," John answered, thinking about how great it would be to hear about someone else's secrets for a change.

The two men pulled their gear out of the back of the truck and went in different directions, as they usually did.

At 4:30, John went to the Ray's truck and waited. At 5:15 he still hadn't shown up. He noticed the foreman leave the office and head to his car. At the last minute, he recognized John and walked over.

"You didn't hear," the foreman said.

"Hear what?" John could tell it was bad news by the way the foreman paused before answering.

"Frozen crust fell on Ray early this afternoon. He didn't have a chance. It was quick. They just finished digging him out. I'm sorry. You need a lift?"

To the foreman, it was just another day at the mines. But John felt like he had been slugged in the stomach. He was still reeling when he approached his porch a few minutes later. Trudging up the stairs, he paused for a moment at the top. A feeling of dread overcame him when he put his hand on the doorknob and heard the sounds of heavy sobbing coming through the door before he opened it.

Ruby, Laverne and three of the kids were in hysterics. The baby was asleep, oblivious to the commotion around him.

After hugging the women, he slid into the kitchen where Laverne cornered him. "These things come in threes, John! First Ruth and now Ray. I'm not going to wait around to find out what the third thing is!"

"Just calm down, dear. It'll be OK."

"Don't you tell me it's going to be OK. It is not going to be OK, goddammit!" she yelled in a whisper without actually raising her voice. "We've got to get out of here. I just want to go home." She started crying again.

"I gotta make a living, hon. I can't just go up to Fort Collins and get new job. We've got four mouths to feed."

The two barely spoke to each other during the next few weeks, and a cloud of uncertainty hung over John and Laverne until fate made their decision for them.

The war had cut gold mining production dramatically, as resources and manpower were diverted for more critical materials and manufacturing. At first, none of this impacted John. But by June, there was talk of the government shutting down all gold production, and John was out of a job. Again.

John offered Ruby $100 for Ray's 1930 Ford Model A Roadster pickup. It was prone to backfiring and it was getting rusty, but Ruby didn't want it any more. She was headed by train to the San Francisco Bay Area to stay with relatives.

Meanwhile, lured by the promise of wartime jobs, most of Laverne's family had recently relocated to Pasadena, California. She thought it sounded like paradise, but John dreaded the thought of being at a crowded dinner table once again, where everyone competed for attention, and where he couldn't figure out how to join a conversation.

But they couldn't stay in Colorado either.

They packed up as much of the house as they could fit into the back of the truck, loaded up the front seat with all four passengers, and headed south to Albuquerque where they joined up with Route 66.

The trip would be nearly 1,200 miles, across New Mexico, Northern Arizona and the Mojave desert. In 1942, travelers had to stop in every single town and plan each gas station visit. If you were the Quinns, you also had to wash diapers every night and figure out how to dry them in a crowded pickup cab.

The family stayed in some of the many western-themed motor courts that lined Route 66, stopping for lunch at a Woolworth's lunch counter or a drug store soda fountain when they could. They were in much better shape than many of the families they saw along the way; folks who had defaulted on their mortgages and lost most of their possessions.

The trip took a bit longer than necessary because John often stopped to help a stranger patch a tire, something he got good at when he drove for the dairy.

One evening there was a heavy thunderstorm that soaked everything in the back of the truck. The canvas cover had blown off. The kids cried all night at the motel, and there were no dry clothes to wear the next day. But Mary got her very own bottle of Bubble Up from a gas station vending machine, and after the initial explosion of sugary foam all over the seat, she was happy.

The old Ford could do 50 mph going downhill, but climbing was much slower. The trip took ten days, with more than one flat tire and an overheated radiator near Flagstaff, Arizona.

After crossing the Cajon Pass near San Bernardino, they saw their first neat rows of tall palm trees lining the streets, sunny groves full of every kind of citrus, Spanish style houses with terra cotta roofs and abundant gardens of bougainvillea, cactus and roses, all under perfect 75°F skies.

Citrus Years in Southern California
Courtesy of Cooper Regional History Museum

The day they arrived was especially clear, due to the infamous Santa Ana winds that blew out all the smog and painted endless views in every direction. The San Gabriel

Mountains ran along the north side of the valleys as they drove west. At 10,000 feet in height, the snowy peaks were reminiscent of Colorado, but without having to drive in them. Perhaps it would be enough just to see the mountains from your porch. Maybe this was paradise after all.

Their mood lightened considerably as they drove the last 20 miles along Foothill Boulevard to Pasadena, to her parents' house.

John turned off the engine and they both took a deep breath.

1942, Southern California

John and Laverne unfolded themselves from the front seat of the pickup truck and stepped onto the grass in front of the apartment. It took some time to get their wobbly legs back to normal, but they were glad to be out of the car and in the land of palm trees and balmy breezes.

Peach Place was a short street with several large apartment buildings behind a row of warehouses in the old section of Pasadena. The apartments were disappointing after passing through the manicured subtropical neighborhoods on the way into town. The monthly rent was $10-$15, and several months earlier, Laverne's parents George and Josephine had snapped up a unit for themselves and their four remaining sons.

John and Laverne arrived just in time for dinner, and no one wasted any time.

"Mom, Dad… John and I are going to look for a place tomorrow. We're happy to sleep on the sofa tonight, if you don't mind. The kids will sleep anyplace," Laverne said.

"No need," George replied. "When I heard that you were moving down here, I checked around and noticed an opening for an apartment next door."

John spoke up. "That was nice, but there's really no need."

"Too late," said George. "You gotta move quickly when you see a vacancy around here. I paid the deposit and signed the paperwork, so you don't need to worry about it."

John discreetly kicked Laverne's leg under the table to register his protest, but she didn't realize the significance. Turning to John, she said, "What was that for?"

"Leg cramp." John hoped his face wasn't turning red with anger and embarrassment. Now he had to commit to an apartment that his father-in-law had already picked out.

Several of Laverne's siblings had married and left the crowded nest by 1942, but sitting at her parents' dining room table felt like she had never left home. She confided in John that she wasn't sure whether the familiarity was good or bad, but she was in awful shape after Cripple Creek, and now she needed some mothering herself.

John hated to admit that it was a relief not having to look for housing after everything they'd been through. After the newness wore off, however, it was back to the old familiar bickering at her parents' dinner table. John and Laverne were feeling smothered, while George and Josephine were acting like parents. Laverne was behaving like a beleaguered teenager.

The apartments were densely occupied, and filled with a continuous drone of loud voices, slamming doors, pounding feet, heated arguments, clearing of throats and what passed for marital bliss at the oddest hours. It reminded John of his early childhood in Manhattan.

Thankfully, John had no luck finding a job. He didn't put it that way, but he didn't really want to find a job that would force him to live on Peach Place in Pasadena for any longer than he had to. He had to make half an effort to appease Laverne and her family, but he was only going through the motions.

After several months of looking around Los Angeles and Pasadena, John convinced Laverne to head to Ontario, a good-sized town about an hour east, at the foot of the mountains. It reminded him a bit of Timnath—close to her family, but not too close.

John had gotten a job as a delivery driver for a freight company, making runs to and from the airport. It was a far cry from his lucrative work in the gold mines, but it was steady, safe and clean.

Ontario was full of long streets lined with craftsman-style bungalows and palm trees. The tall mountains were only a few miles away, and on clear days they were a welcome distraction from the drudgery of the work.

John and Laverne's third child came a short time later, and they named her Ruth, after Laverne's recently departed sister. She even looked like her.

Mary and little John had budding personalities and made friends in the neighborhood, even if John and Laverne barely knew any of their neighbors.

Things were good at work until a co-worker loudly complained that John had "Jewed him" out of an easier delivery route. John was offended for more than one reason and took a swing at the guy, who turned out to be the boss' son-in-law.

John lost his job, and everything got bad after that—both financially and in their marriage. They had used up most of their savings from the Cripple Creek years, and they were struggling.

"John," Laverne said with a bitter undertone one evening.

"What." John asked, sounding more like a statement.

"We should never have left Pasadena,"

"There was nothing there for me, you know that," John replied.

"Oh, come on John. LA's a big town. Not a single job? And now we're out here almost an hour away from our nearest friends?"

"Really? We didn't have friends in Pasadena. We had your folks."

"Well, at least we'd have a sitter if I needed to go get a job. What kind of place is this, where nobody knows who lives next door?"

"And whose fault is that? What do you do all day while I'm at work?"

Laverne slammed her magazine onto the coffee table. "We have three kids, in case you haven't noticed. And what's wrong with my family anyway? You've had a problem with them since the beginning. And don't tell me you haven't."

"Well, what's wrong with *me?* Isn't living in Ontario with *me* good enough? You never really wanted to leave home, did you? Why don't you admit it?"

John couldn't stand the way Laverne was looking at him at that moment. He could only imagine what was going on in her mind. It was just as well, because she was wondering if she should have married the first man she ever kissed.

Meanwhile, John was feeling like his life was doomed by bad break after bad break.

Leaving New York because of Pat, losing the sandblaster job, old man Conway selling the farm, the dairy going belly up, Ray dying, the mines closing. And now this asshole at work. None of that was my fault. None of it. I never had a chance, John fumed to himself. *But I always put food on the table.*

The Quinns avoided each other for the rest of the evening and into the next morning. John thought of one last option as he drank his coffee.

"The draft board hasn't called my number."

"You're not serious."

"Yes, I am. It's a paycheck. You can move back to Pasadena while I'm gone."

"We don't know how long that will be."

"That's right. We don't."

Laverne grabbed a Kleenex and dabbed her eye as she looked out the window, knowing that he might never come home.

A few days later, she gave him a kiss goodbye at Union Station in downtown LA. He said "I love you" as she was turning away, but he couldn't tell if she heard him or not. She left before he boarded the train with his head hanging low.

The following week, Laverne took the kids and moved back to Pasadena to be near her folks.

1944–1945, Germany

A few days earlier at the the Los Angeles recruiting office, John was worried where he would end up in the Army as a 35 year old with no special skills. He wondered how much he could enhance his background without being too obvious:

Education: 1 year of high school

It's only an extra year of school, but it sounds better than 8th grade.

Civil Occupation: Policemen and Detectives

That sounds good. I did do some work around police in New York, right? But if they ask, it was detective work for Ray's company, who's not around to verify it anyway.

It didn't matter. John went to boot camp for several weeks like everyone else. Before he knew it, he was on an eastbound transport train for the east coast.

A few days later, he stood on Pier 88 at the edge of the New York skyline, with the sights and sounds of midtown Manhattan as the backdrop. He closed his eyes and listened to the hordes of honking taxis mixing with laughing seagulls.

It made him smile. In front of him was the Queen Mary, which was painted a dull solid grey in order to avoid the German navy.

John was only a few miles from Jersey City, across the Hudson River. *Would my parents be proud?* he wondered.

The line of troops began to move, and the boarding process began.

The next morning, they sailed out of New York harbor, past the Statue of Liberty, and behind it, Jersey City. He didn't know if or when he would see it again.

Two years earlier, Hitler had offered a bounty of $250,000 and the Iron Cross medal to any U-boat commander who could sink the ship. As a result, standard procedure was to take a zig-zag course across the Atlantic, changing direction at regular intervals to make a more difficult target.

The constant turning meant that the ship tilted sickeningly 24 hours a day. The Queen Mary didn't have enough bunks, so the men slept in three eight-hour shifts.

A week later, the ship finally docked at Gourock, Scotland. John moved to a series of bases in England before ultimately being sent to the beaches of France, where the massive Normandy invasion had taken place only a few weeks earlier.

As part of the Sixth Army Group, he saw little action until he was in Alsace, France, on the German border. Then things got hairy. His battalion sustained heavy casualties under constant bombardment.

There were days when John and the men around him were coated in so much mud that the whites of their eyes and teeth were the only betrayal of their camouflage.

John made and lost a few friends in his company. They were guys from all over the country, but his closest pals usually had similar accents to his. GIs often listened for signs of where someone was from, and they enjoyed sharing familiar stories of home. After all, the population of the US was still heavily weighted toward the northeast during the second world war, and New York sent more soldiers to battle than any other state.

One night amidst the chaos of battle during a thunderstorm, John became separated from his group. He collapsed into a bomb crater to catch his bearings during a lull in the fighting. Bullets whizzed over his head and flares lit up the sky. Another GI fell into the hole with him and they lifted the fronts of their helmets in mutual acknowledgement. It wasn't anybody that he recognized.

John asked the other soldier if he had a match, and when he leaned over to get a light, he noticed a pretty bad burn scar on the guy's hand. It reminded him of someone he used to know, but he couldn't remember who it was.

The GI asked John if he could bum a smoke, and John heard an unmistakable New York accent.

John was about to ask him where he was from, when a flare lit up the sky and he suddenly realized he was in a hole with Gus, his old boss, who wanted to avenge Pat Duffy's death. Gus—the man who pulled him into an

Irish crime family and then chased after him 16 years ago. *How the hell?*

John knew he had to do something quickly, before Gus figured out who he was. He discreetly pulled the bayonet off his rifle. When a flicker of recognition moved across Gus' face, John instinctively pinned him to the muddy incline and held the blade to his neck.

It wasn't clear what he should to do next, but he couldn't let Gus make the next move.

The two men stared at each other as John talked shakily. "I didn't mean to kill him, you know. It was dark, and I thought I was shooting the other guy. I was trying to help him. It was an accident."

"So now you're gonna kill me too?" Gus asked.

"I can't let you go. I'm not going to prison for Pat. Not now. But I gotta ask—how did you figure out it was me that night? No one saw Pat and me leave for Jersey. I looked."

Gus laughed in his face.

John glared at him and pressed the sharp edge closer to Gus's jugular vein. "You think this is funny?"

"You were never that bright, were ya kid."

"I was 19," John said, even as he remembered that he was actually only 15.

"You were a fucking idiot. I saw you and Pat that night at the warehouse," Gus said.

"No way. I was behind a bunch of stacked crates."

"I was the snitch Pat was after. He killed one of my guys that night, one of my cops, and he was gonna kill me next. I was the guy who shot him."

"No, Gus—I fired at you several times, but I didn't know it was you. One of my shots hit Pat instead."

"That's right, pal. You shot at me, and you were a lousy aim. I grabbed Pat's gun, and I didn't miss. I saw you standing there when I took off."

"So I didn't kill him?" John was stunned. He replayed the events of that night several times in his head.

"As soon as you started shooting, you were the perfect cover. I was happy to let you take the heat for Pat. I figured you'd run home to mommy in Jersey City and I'd never see you again. I got Pat's territory, and I had police coverage to boot."

John was relieved, but filled with crazy anger at himself for being such an idiot.

After 16 years of looking over his shoulder, he had ruined his life. He left school in the eight grade. His parents were presumably crushed. He thought he was a murderer for all these years. Shit job after shit job, and now it was all a joke? And the joke was on him? Rage coursed through John's veins.

"Are you fucking kidding me? I ought to slice your weasel throat for fucking up my life."

"Look. No one is after you. Let it go. You really want to go to prison for this? Now?"

John pressed the blade against Gus's neck again, breaking the skin a bit, until he heard a voice in the darkness behind him.

"OK listen up, men. We're moving out. Grab your gear. Let's go."

John released the knife from its intended target, but kept his eyes locked on Gus to be sure he didn't try anything.

Holy shit. I didn't do it, John said under his breath. He had replayed Pat's death so many times over the years that the low hum of shame and guilt had become his constant companions. Now he didn't even know who he was anymore.

As a soldier, he'd been shooting at bad guys for months and felt absolutely no remorse. But one accidental shooting of a criminal — something he didn't even do — could alter the course of his life for years. It made no sense.

Gus shook his head with contempt and walked away into the night. John was unable to move for a few minutes until the blood resumed pumping into his brain and he felt a rifle butt nudge against his shoulder. "Come on, move it soldier. Let's go."

The next couple of months were a blur, as his unit worked its way through town after town, past Stuttgart and across Bavaria, toward Munich. He hadn't heard from home in nearly a month, but the mail caught up with him all at once, when he was relieved to get four newsy letters from Laverne.

John never saw Gus again. He had relatively little recollection of this period until he found himself on the outskirts of Munich in April of 1945, at a concentration camp called Dachau.

What John saw sliced through his youthful bravado of the past decade and a half. Emaciated prisoners. Piles of dead bodies. An overpowering stench. Crematorium stacks.

This wasn't a military prison. These were civilians. They were mostly Jews.

John had both a visceral reaction and an inexplicable sense of detachment as his mind raced.

Are these my people? Are any of them my relatives? Am I even Jewish any more? Or is it in my blood, like a permanent tattoo? Did Laverne suspect anything? Why was she was so cold when I left? Did her father tell her that he suspected?

His hand reached into his shirt and clutched the St. Christopher medal that Laverne had given him just before he shipped off, as if it would somehow make him more Catholic.

Who am I kidding? His fingers ran over St. Christopher's face, unsure of its power.

He slid into a small warehouse to catch his breath for a few moments. He rubbed his eyelids with his knuckles and took a few deep breaths, but when he opened his eyes, he noticed that the quiet room was filled almost to the brim with empty suitcases. Most of them had names written on them: Levi, Hoffman, Abrams, Cohen, Rosen, Klein, Blum. These were the names of his youth; his neighbors, his classmates, and the people who stood around him in the synagogue.

Near the bottom of the pile was a worn and scratched leather suitcase with the name KATZ neatly printed in the center.

John quickly stepped outside again and moved around the camp, but the dead and the living skeletons were everywhere he turned. There was no getting away from them. He started to imagine Sam and Minnie with their faces superimposed on the victims, pleading with him for food, their bony hands outstretched, competing with him for air.

The eyes and mouths of the dead inmates were half open, as if they were watching him and trying to say something.

What Jewish or Catholic god would allow this kind of hell on earth?

His mind was racing in circles, like he was on a playground merry-go-round, spinning faster and faster. Nausea rose in his stomach.

GIs around him were holding tears back. Photographers documented everything. Generals spoke into microphones. But John was numb. There was no emotion except the sensation that his mind was a turntable needle being ripped across a vinyl record. Someone spoke into his ear, but it was his own voice. His body wasn't his to command anymore. He got dizzy, vomited and blacked out.

When he woke up, he was in a hospital near Frankfurt. He was diagnosed with Shell Shock Syndrome, and had been heavily medicated. The drugs might have made things worse, because nightmares increasingly kept him awake most nights. The nurses then gave him something to make him sleep, but the high doses made him groggy most days. Somehow in the medicated haze, he had missed the end of the war. After several weeks he stabilized, and it was time to go home.

An overcrowded troop ship took him to New York once again, and he got a lump in this throat as the Statue of Liberty slid past, standing guard in front of Jersey City. It was bittersweet to be back in New York, but he just wanted to go home to Laverne and the kids. There were still 3,000 miles between him and his own pillow. He didn't set foot outside, except to hail a cab from Pier 90 to Penn Station, where he caught the first available fast train to the west coast, after waiting in the lobby for six hours.

Settling into a window seat, his train soon emerged from the Hudson River tunnel into New Jersey. He felt sadness and regret as he thought about his parents and his family again, who were only a mile away at that very moment—so close, yet so far. He pressed his face to the glass as he strained to see the neon lights of Journal Square.

Have they forgotten me by now? Is everyone still alive? Willie is probably a successful engineer by now. I'm shit. That's what I am. I'm shit.

A kindly grandmother sat across the aisle, knitting. She smiled at him, but he hoped that she wouldn't make small talk. He closed his eyes and pretended to sleep.

He wondered again if he should write a quick postcard just to let his folks know that he served in the war and came back, but decided, as his father used to say, that he should let sleeping dogs lie.

Besides, I'm doomed to be a nobody. I do manual labor working for other people. You'd be ashamed if you could see me now. Especially after I figured out that it was all for nothing.

Maybe I should have been killed in the war, because then I'd at least be a hero.

As the train rolled toward Pennsylvania, he noticed hobos hiding in the bushes outside the smaller stations, waiting to hop a passing freight train. He was in a deluxe passenger train this time, but he felt like a bum.

He could clearly visualize the young kid running for the train; the one whose life he couldn't save, and the hopeful look on the boy's face in the last seconds of his life.

There was also his friend Lou, who had dreamt of a better life in Oregon. He couldn't save him either.

Then he thought of Bessie Thompson and the others who helped him along the way. He remembered Ray and Ruby, and Ruth and her baby.

He pondered his own children. They were his flesh and blood, whether that blood was Jewish or Irish Catholic. They knew nothing of his failures, and to them, John was their one and only father.

Maybe the pain of the last 16 years was for no good reason, but he got a wife and kids during that time. If he hadn't lost his job in Pittsburgh, he might not have headed west. If Lou hadn't died on the train, then John wouldn't have gotten off at LaSalle, and he wouldn't have met Laverne. She came along just in time.

Maybe everything happens for a reason, he concluded. The sudden realization that he truly loved Laverne took him by surprise.

Just then, a young boy passing in the aisle saluted when he saw John sitting in his uniform. A row of American flags somewhere in central Pennsylvania made him feel proud. He felt defeated and victorious at the same time.

Surviving the war was one thing, but now it was time to go back to his old life and try to make something of himself, before it was too late.

1945, Southern California

Laverne and the kids came to greet the train when it pulled into downtown LA. The kids ran and jumped into his arms, although Ruth didn't quite remember him. Laverne gave him a long-awaited tearful kiss and an "I love you too" before they drove home.

After a week back on Peach Place in Pasadena, it was like John had never left, but in a good way. Laverne seemed genuinely happy to see him. Even old man Conway was smiling now and then.

Like many other men coming home from the war, John didn't discuss it in any great depth. He could recite the places he had been, but the rest of his experience was sparsely explained.

His daughter Mary, now eight years old, asked if he had killed any Nazis.

"Sure, a few."

"Did you see any dead people?"

"No, not a lot," he lied.

"Were you scared?"

"Not too bad." Another lie.

"Grandpa says they killed a lot of Jews."

It surprised John that she'd already heard about this. "Yes, that's right, honey."

"I sure am glad we're not Jews."

"Hey it's time for bed, princess."

Out of the corner of his eye, John saw George Conway standing just beyond the kitchen doorway, listening to the conversation. George looked at him blankly, his expression impossible to read.

John stood up and went down the hall to tuck Mary in, trying to ignore the ghosts of Dachau.

After living with her parents for the last 18 months, Laverne was more than ready to leave. A few months earlier, a vagrant was arrested after repeatedly sleeping in her car that was parked across the street. She worried for the safety of her young family. They went back out to Ontario, and John got a job as a driver again, this time working for various growers and shippers of oranges.

The work was steady, if unexciting, and things felt stable for the first time in years.

Living in Ontario had its perks, too. When the air was clear, the scenes looked just like the ones on orange crate labels in the grocery stores.

Every Fourth of July, there was an All States Picnic, in which people from every state in the union got together and sat at the world's longest picnic table—a mile long—in the median divide of Euclid Avenue, under dozens of pepper trees. One year, a record 120,000 picnickers showed up and ate cold chicken and watermelon with transplants from their home states.

Citrus label collection, Courtesy of The Huntington Library
San Marino, California

John and his family sat at the Colorado tables, and met up with a few of Laverne's high school friends from Wellington. He went out of his way to avoid the New Jersey table, which was thankfully half a mile away.

After joining the American Legion, he became active in many volunteer events. His knack for details was obvious, and he became useful in organizing resources and finances for the local post.

As parents of three kids, they went to PTA meetings and had birthday parties and decorated their house for Halloween.

Every March, Laverne put up shamrocks and leprechauns around the house, and they toasted his late parents, John and Mary Quinn.

Once in a while, the children would ask about their Irish grandparents and about his life as a child in New York.

One evening in 1947, after they went to bed, Laverne asked him, "When we have enough money, dear, I want you to take me to New York to see where you grew up. Don't you want to see it again?"

"Well, after my parents died, I lived across the river in Jersey City with a foster family."

"How old were you when you left New Jersey?"

John did the math in his head. "Oh, I guess about 18."

"Well then, you can take me to Jersey City too."

"Maybe someday, Laverne."

Later that night, while John was halfway between thinking and dreaming, he heard his father's voice just behind his right ear. Over the years, he had forgotten what it sounded like. It was definitely Sam's voice, and his mouth was moving but the words were indistinct. The only thing that John could make out was "Isadore," which his father repeated several times. It was like Sam was trying to tell him something, but it was impossible to decipher what it was.

The dream seemed very real, and it lingered with him for a long time.

John and Laverne settled into a routine, and John took on more and more volunteer work. He was home for supper every night, and the kids knew their father. They had days at the beach, stopping at Knott's Berry farm on the way home for fried chicken and boysenberry pie. Once in a while they went into LA to go to the La Brea tar pits or a show.

By the early 1950s, citrus was having a big decline, not only from disease, but from a massive building boom in the suburbs east of Los Angeles.

Orange groves fell by the square mile, replaced by tract homes, shopping centers and new schools. John could see that his citrus driving days were coming to an end. During one period, this area was the world's largest producer of oranges, but now the citrus industry was only a small vestige of its glory days.

John thought about finding another driving job, but decided he was ready for a change.

"I'm tired of sitting on my ass all day. For once, I want to make a job change before I have to."

"What are you thinking about?"

One thing that was booming in those years was the restaurant business, as more people had disposable income, and women increasingly worked outside the home. John wondered if this might be a good time to change professions, but first he needed to get some cooking experience.

"Restaurants."

"Oh, John. Long hours. Nights and weekends"

"I'll try to find a day job, if I can."

Laverne sighed, knowing it would be tough to change John's mind. "OK, but let's get one thing straight. You come home smelling like greasy fries and you're sleeping on the sofa. Got it?"

His first food-related job was as a cooking assistant at the Pacific Colony State Hospital in Spadra. Hiring more food staff was part of a shift from housing the "feeble-minded" to serving "clients."

Once they learned that John understood the purchase order process, they asked him to work most of the time in the business office, and only a few hours in the kitchen. It wasn't what he had in mind. Instead of learning about cooking, he was tracking down missing napkin orders, and calling around for vast quantities of ground beef.

John had no interaction with the patients, but one day he needed to walk through a ward to do an errand. He became overwhelmed with the sensation that everyone around him was an inmate in a concentration camp. This time he couldn't put them out of his mind. Some of the patients were restrained to their beds. Their gaunt and ghostly faces were the same ones he had seen less than ten years earlier, when he was part of the liberation team. His heart began to race and his mind replayed some of the horrific sounds and smells of that day. The urge to jump over everyone's head and escape was overpowering.

John walked to the back of the ward, through the security door, and out to his car where he sat for ten minutes to regain his composure. He quit the next morning.

There was a friend from the American Legion lodge, who ran a New York-style delicatessen in nearby Covina, and John gave him a call. It turned out that he needed help, as he was about to go on a long overdue vacation. John could learn about the restaurant business, and then they would talk about a longer term role as a business partner when his pal came back.

Traffic would make the drive from Ontario a challenge every morning, but his friend knew of someone who had an old farm house in an ancient orange grove in West Covina. The house and the trees were due to be demolished for the new San Bernardino Freeway. Four to six lanes would run right through the property, but it would likely be another year or so before construction began on this stretch. John and his family could stay there for as long as they wanted, practically for free, and eat all the oranges they could pick.

The Quinn family moved into an old white clapboard farm house along Garvey Avenue in West Covina, surrounded by acres of gnarled orange trees.

The kids had fun climbing the branches and throwing rotten oranges at each other. Laverne lined the drawers and cupboards with flowery paper, and made curtains to block the view of the busy road in front of the house.

That same week, John began working at the Corned Beef King in downtown Covina, a town whose motto was "A Mile Square and All There."

As he would soon find out, it takes a while to get the hang of dealing with customers.

Covina, California
University of Southern Calif. Libraries and Calif. Historical Society

1955, Covina, CA

John Quinn had lived up to this point without managing to run into any of his old relatives, who he presumed had all stayed in New York and New Jersey. Unbeknownst to him, his oldest sister, Lil, and her husband moved to Los Angeles in the 1950s.

Her son, Richard, the baby nephew who Isadore Katz had made faces with at his parents' dinner table so many years ago, got married and moved to West Covina. He ended up less than a mile from the farm house John was living in—3,000 miles from where they last saw each other.

One night John's and Richard's paths crossed, but neither of them realized it.

This chance meeting probably wouldn't have happened, except that Richard's pregnant wife had a hankering for corned beef on rye that evening. Or maybe just ice cream. Or both. Or a cheeseburger. No—a corned beef, with Russian dressing on the side. And a pickle. Then she dared him to surprise her, which was like playing 20 questions, only there was never a right answer. Just a spin of the roulette wheel, randomly resulting in her approval or disappointment.

They were both exhausted, and it was getting late. They'd just moved into a brand new ranch-style tract house in West Covina, and there were boxes everywhere. Dinner wouldn't be coming out of that kitchen for at least several days.

"I hope I can find a place that's open," he said, feeling pessimistic as he grabbed his keys.

As he drove along the dark rows of old orange trees and turned left onto Citrus Avenue, Richard couldn't let go of the nagging realization that buying a new house for $13,900 in the middle of nowhere probably wasn't a smart idea. Maybe his mother was right, and they should've stayed in their tiny LA rental. After all, the family came from a long line of urban apartment dwellers, which is how ordinary folks lived back in New Jersey and New York.

Only a month ago, he'd bought a two-toned persimmon and black '55 Studebaker Commander, which turned a lot of heads, but was also an extravagance at $2,000. "What the hell was I thinking" he mumbled, more as a statement than a question, surprised that he was now having conversations with himself out loud.

His firstborn kid was due in a few months, and his sales commission checks weren't exactly predictable. What a mess.

The math was still churning in his head when he realized that he was standing at the counter of the Corned Beef King, a tiny outpost of New York deli food in the barren wasteland of Wonder Bread and Velveeta that was suburban LA during the Eisenhower years.

In front of him, with his hands on the counter, was an impatient-looking guy with an east coast accent, who sniped, "We close at eight."

Richard was so tired and preoccupied that he didn't even remember driving there or getting out of the car. The buzzing fluorescent lights were competing with Sinatra, who was in the back singing "Jeepers Creepers." The deli guy brushed past him and unplugged the neon red OPEN sign, as if to make a point.

"Yeah okay—two corned beef sandwiches, Russian on the side. And a pickle."

"Sorry, no sandwiches. Meat's put away already. We're about to close."

"Isn't this the Corned Beef King?"

John threw him an *oh, a wise guy* look, flaring his nostrils with contempt

"I haven't turned off the soup yet. It's chicken soup," he offered, softening his demeanor a bit. Richard nodded, unable to think of an alternative quickly enough.

After John opened the soup lid, Richard caught a whiff of what smelled exactly like his grandma Minnie's chicken soup. She always used the leafy celery tops in the broth, which exuded an authenticity that only a Jewish grandmother would know about.

For a few moments, he pictured the brick duplex with bay windows on Fulton Avenue in Jersey City that he'd left several years earlier. His grandparents, Sam and Minnie, had lived in the downstairs unit, while Richard and his family lived upstairs since the early 1930s. His aunts, uncles and cousins still lived back East, but Richard came to Southern California like so many Navy guys did after the war, and decided to stay. He was proud that he was the first member of his family to get out of New Jersey. Several years later, his parents moved west.

He wondered how Minnie was doing. She'd been a widow now for 8 years, and the last time he saw her before getting on the bus to California, she actually puddled up. She didn't cry when he joined the Navy at age 17 and left for the U-Boat war in the Atlantic, but for some reason, this move felt more permanent to her.

Meanwhile, John was ladling the soup, and thinking of how much it reminded him of the way his mother, Minnie, used to make it, with leafy celery tops, when he lived in the brick duplex on Fulton Avenue in Jersey City.

He hadn't thought of his mother or his boyhood home for a while. It was another life, really. Someone else's life.

He brought the paper bag out front and handed it to his customer. They studied each other's face for a fleeting moment, as if there was a vague familiarity, but they both dismissed it. Between the soup, and Sinatra crooning about "The Wee Small Hours" on the radio, they each had a pang of nostalgia for the New Jersey of their childhoods.

"So long," they both said at precisely the same time, and in the same musical tone.

They chuckled about it in perfect unison as Richard leaned against the swinging door on the way out, trying not to spill the soup. Then they laughed together once again because of how ridiculously identical the first laugh was.

OK, that was weird, they both thought, completely unaware of the collision of memories that had just transpired.

Richard drove off into the night. *Crap, she wanted corned beef. I can hear it now. I wonder where I can find ice cream at this hour.*

John closed up shop. *What a dump. I gotta get out of here. I need to work in a real restaurant. Only a few more days until Bill gets back.*

* * *

Richard and his family lived in their new home for 20 years.

John moved on from the Corned Beef King, and got a job at a family restaurant about five miles away. He worked there for a long time—as an assistant, as a chef, and eventually as a manager. He tried to be home for dinner most nights, but weekends were tough.

After moving his family to a neighboring town, they were able to buy a small house very close to the foothills. When he stepped out of his front door and looked to the right, the mountains seemed to grow steeply out of nowhere, like an exotic backdrop at the end of the street.

On crisp winter mornings after a storm, the mountains would be covered in snow, but it could still be 70 degrees at the house, and his orange tree and bougainvillea would be thriving.

John's children went to high school, and he continued with his volunteer activities, which got an increasing amount of attention from the local small town newspaper. There were meetings, luncheons and fundraisers, parades and ceremonies.

The first few times his photo appeared in the paper, he was a little uneasy. He had spent nearly a lifetime trying to avoid being recognized, but now he enjoyed the attention, and it eventually became a source of pride.

It felt pretty good to finally be a somebody.

1960, Jersey City, NJ

Laverne finally convinced John to take her to New York during the spring. They had the money and the vacation time. The kids had graduated, except for Ruth who was still a junior, but who would stay with one of Laverne's sisters nearby.

It would be their first plane trip. They flew from Los Angeles to New York's Idyllwild International in a silver American Airlines 707 Astrojet. During the descent, John could see his old neighborhood out the window by tracing the park and old houses closest to the Statue of Liberty and then counting west. He had just about spotted Fulton Avenue between the major boulevards when low clouds got in the way.

The Quinns spent the next few days seeing the usual sights. They saw shows, went to museums, window-shopped on Fifth Avenue, and John took her to an automat for mac and cheese and baked beans. He had more vivid memories than he could permit himself to share with her, but he was happy to be there.

They rode in a carriage through Central Park and marveled at the blossoms that were beginning to appear on the trees.

John noticed the steam coming from the tops of the buildings. The din of traffic, sirens and honking taxis didn't annoy him. They were strangely soothing.

He never hated New York, and at night as he was falling asleep, he thought about what he'd be doing right now if he hadn't left home—where would he live, who would he be married to, what would his profession be.

The night before they were due to go home, Laverne asked why he hadn't taken her past any of the places he lived.

"What about when you lived in Manhattan?"

"I honestly don't remember the address. It was on East 49th, but I couldn't tell you the address or which building. I'm sure it's gone by now."

"What about Jersey City? You didn't leave there until you were 18."

John did the math in his head. He had left over 30 years ago. The old place would be too big for Sam and Minnie, if they were still around. They would be in a much smaller apartment by now, without an upstairs. Still, it's not like the Quinns would walk inside the place.

How bad could a drive-by be?

"Fine. We'll go tomorrow. I'll take you past my foster family's home on Fulton."

John thought he would dread it, but he didn't. He was looking forward to seeing his street and his house. He might even go past his old school.

As they came through the Holland Tunnel, John thought about his bus trip into Manhattan that day in 1928 when he ran away from home. Then he remembered the drive to Jersey in Pat Duffy's car, and the panicked return trip back to the city later that night.

These memories stayed locked inside his head, but it seemed like everywhere he turned was the scene of yet another untellable story from his past. It was frustrating.

They drove down the leafy part of Hudson County Boulevard and turned left onto Fulton Avenue. John parked the car on the other side of the street.

Isadore and his family lived on the ground floor on the left
Image © Google Maps

In front of the duplex was a For Sale sign. Who knows how many families had lived in the apartment since he was last here, he wondered.

They got out of the car, and John talked about where his old school was, which neighbors lived in which houses, and pointed to the bedroom window that was his.

Suddenly a light came on in the front of the apartment, in the bay window. He froze as a woman appeared in the middle of the room. She seemed to be sweeping or vacuuming the floor.

That can't be my mother, John said to himself. *She would be almost 80.* This woman's movements were way too brisk.

She must have seen John and Laverne standing out front, because she disappeared for a moment and then the front door opened. John held his breath, but thankfully it was a stranger.

"Can I help you? The open house isn't until Sunday. I'm just getting it ready. I'm sorry I can't let you in."

John muttered something about having lived there long ago, and the woman said, "Oh—did you know Minnie?"

His heart skipped a beat. "No, why?"

"She lived here for many years. Passed away a few weeks ago. The family's eager to sell the place."

"Sorry, doesn't ring a bell," John replied. His eyes welled up unexpectedly as he turned away so Laverne couldn't see him. After a few seconds that seemed like minutes, he pointed to a bus stop across the boulevard.

"That's where my foster dad used to get off the bus from work." He blew his nose with a handkerchief. "I'd forgotten how bad the pollen is here."

Turning to the lady standing at the top of the stairs, he waved, "Thanks, and good luck with the sale."

John got into the car without opening the door for Laverne, for the first time in their relationship. He stared emptily at the equator in the center of the decorative blue globe in the middle of the chrome horn ring inside the steering wheel of the Oldsmobile that he had rented. Laverne climbed in beside him.

"John, where are your foster parents? What happened to them? You never discuss them."

"There's something I never told you." John continued to look down. He needed to spill at least some of his story. "I ran away from home. I wasn't 18. I was 14."

Laverne raised her eyebrows. "You ran away from this home?"

"Yes. And I never let them know I was OK. And I always felt bad about it." John felt a lump rise in his throat again.

"Why did you leave?"

"They had too many kids, and I was the youngest. I didn't belong to them. They were Jewish. I was an outsider, as were most of the kids living there. They were in it for the money."

"John, was Minnie your foster mother?"

There was silence as he thought about his answer.

Laverne could finally hear the whole sordid story at that very moment. He could tell her the truth, but that would make him and their family a lie; his Irish heritage, his religion, the names of two of his children named after his Irish parents—hell, his own name, John—the Catholic school his oldest daughter went to, the annual holiday rituals. Not to mention that old man Conway's worst suspicions would be confirmed, and that would poison Laverne forever. John would lose his family.

No, he decided. The real story would be taken to his grave. The short term relief he would enjoy right now wouldn't be worth the hell he would endure in explaining the lies his family was living with for all these years.

"Yes, Minnie was my foster mother. She was something."

"But I'm your wife. Why didn't you tell me? Why did you wait until now? And why did you tell the lady you didn't know her?"

"Because I was in the eighth grade when I left. I was embarrassed, and then ashamed as time went on."

She seemed to accept his answer, even though she still didn't understand how he made his way in the world as a 14-year-old kid, or much of what he did before he met her. *How old was he now? Now was not the time to push it,* she decided.

They returned to their hotel in Manhattan, and that night when it was time to get ready for bed, John closed the bathroom door and cried quietly as he ran water in the sink.

They returned home the next day, after a quiet flight over Pennsylvania and Colorado. John could easily make out the ugly gash of the gold mines in Cripple Creek as he pictured Ruth's and Ray's faces.

* * *

In the coming years, John rededicated himself to focus on community service activities that benefitted children, and in particular, at-risk boys. He worked his way up the ranks of the American Legion as commander and local Red Cross as chairman. He was involved in fundraising for the Drug Abuse Council, the area Boy Scout council, the parks and recreation department, blood drives and others. They supported a high school that accommodated kids who needed to work while finishing their high school diplomas. They awarded scholarships.

John's knack for being resourceful served him well. When he retired early, he was able to devote more time to public service work. He was the master of ceremonies for countless events, giving speeches and winning accolades for his commitment to the community.

His children married and had families of their own, but they lived nearby, so they got together often. John and Laverne stayed in the same house for another 20 years. You might say they lived happily ever after.

One evening, after appearing in a newspaper story about his role as a model citizen, Laverne needled him about becoming famous. It snuck up on him later in life than he expected, but John finally realized that he had made peace with himself and his accomplishments.

He wondered about his siblings.

Did any of them make it to California, even as tourists? If they were sitting in the next car at a traffic light, would I still recognize them? Would they recognize me?

He wished them well, wherever they were.

1980, Southern California

One warm Sunday in the summer of 1980, John pulled together a last-minute barbecue in his backyard. The entire family was there, including his grandchildren. They weren't celebrating a special occasion—it was just an overdue gathering. The late-day sea breeze cooled things off while the kids chased each other and the grownups tossed horseshoes. It was a perfect evening.

Afterwards, Laverne told him she'd clean up the rest, and to go inside and relax. He went to bed earlier than usual.

He had overeaten, but falling asleep was easy. Within minutes, he dreamt that he was crossing the street in front of his old home on Fulton Avenue in Jersey City.

A car honked as it swerved to avoid hitting him. AOOOO-GAH. The driver yelled, "Idiot!" gesturing with his arm out the window.

"Wow—that's a classic Model T. You don't see many of those anymore," John marveled to himself.

The house looked wonderful—better than it looked in 1960 when he was there with Laverne. He stared at the building, and his gaze became fixed on the large front door. It was hot and muggy, and the air was thick with the sound of buzzing cicadas.

He smelled his mom's roses next to the fence. A piano was playing Debussy's "Clair de Lune" in the upstairs apartment where the music teacher lived. A biplane sputtered low and slow, dodging summertime clouds in the hazy New Jersey sky.

One of his old neighbors waved from their porch. "Hiya Izzie! How ya been?" John nodded and smiled as he approached the steps.

His hand slid up the familiar rail next to the stairs—the same rail he used to ride as a shortcut down to the sidewalk. He stood at the top of the stoop for a moment and wondered if he should knock. A whiff of roast chicken wafted past his nose. There was laughter and conversation inside.

After remembering that he was having a dream, he decided it was OK to dispense with formalities. He opened the door and stood once again in the hallway in front of the old family photo. There he was at age seven, right in the middle, squished between his parents. He grinned and turned toward the dining room.

Everyone stopped talking and jumped up to greet him. They surrounded and hugged him without judgement.

"Isadore! Where have you been?" Sam asked, smiling.

Minnie was crying. "Oh, thank God! We didn't know if you were dead or alive." She ran over and kissed him repeatedly.

Willie approached and hugged him. "I missed you."

Lou and Harry and Lil surrounded him with their arms. "We all missed you. We knew you'd be back."

Sam gestured to an empty chair. "Sit down. Tell us what you've been up to."

Isadore took his seat and didn't know where to begin. They all looked exactly like they did when he left home in 1928. It was hard to know how much they needed to hear, but he had their full attention. Every single one of them. It felt good.

He began to talk, but suddenly he realized two sisters were missing. "Hey, where are Jean and Shirley?"

They all looked at each other and waited for Sam to speak. "They're not here yet. They'll be here later. Go on."

Isadore resumed telling as much of his story as he could remember.

When he got to the part about moving to Cripple Creek in 1940, Willie smiled like he knew the punchline. "Yes, that was a rough couple of years, wasn't it? he observed.

Isadore continued, although he was confused by Willie's comment. He talked about the war, and the realistic dream he had in 1947 about Sam.

Sam smiled. "I could finally see you, but you couldn't see me. It was so frustrating. I tried."

Isadore was puzzled, but he kept talking, and they all listened.

There was the story of when he came to this duplex in 1960, shortly after Minnie died.

Now it was her turn to laugh out loud. "You thought I was that cleaning lady in the window. And I thought you were going to faint when the door opened!"

"Yes, I did. How did you know? Hey, what's going on here?" Isadore asked.

"You don't need to tell us the rest. We already know," Harry said, looking around at the others.

"Wait—I don't get it. I know I'm dreaming, but is it 1928 or 1980?"

"It's 1980 of course," Lil said.

Isadore turned to his mother. "But Mom, you died 20 years ago. You're all so young here. What about you, Pop? When did you, um…?"

"1947," Sam replied with a wink.

"I went first, in 1940. Fourth of July," Willie said. "I've been watching you the longest."

"1967," said Lou. "I missed all the action."

"1974 for me," Lil said. "We only lived 20 miles apart when I moved to LA. We were practically neighbors!"

Harry spoke up. "1977. It seems like just yesterday."

Isadore suddenly realized that Jean and Shirley weren't there yet because they were still alive. Then why was he here?

"But if you all knew what happened to me, why did you make me tell it again?"

"My dear son," Sam said. "It wasn't enough for us to know your story. You've been waiting for over 50 years to tell it to us, freely, in your own words. You needed to do this. We're so very proud of you."

"Mom. Pop. Please forgive me.. I'm so sorry.. I didn't..," Isadore said, his eyes welling up with regret, as he felt every cell in his body come alive in a wave of awareness and clarity.

All the scenes in his life, ending with the ones of Laverne and the kids in California, came rushing back in a flood of vivid memories.

He stood up, but his feet didn't touch the floor. Moving toward the big bay window, he looked over his shoulder at his family.

Everyone smiled at him lovingly and nodded as the light got brighter and faded into white.

Epilogue

This story isn't intended to change who John was to his second family, or to diminish his accomplishments. He was a husband, a parent, a grandfather and a civic role model, with or without his past.

If anything, I respected him more after recognizing the kinds of challenges he faced as a young man. He made his way without a high school education, skills or work experience. He was there for the Great Depression, the Great Drought, the Second World War, and the premature deaths of young people around him.

His success came not from his paycheck, but from what he accomplished in his later years, when he was a "somebody" at last, and in a position to give something back.

We'll never know the real reasons why Isadore left home in 1928. He would not have been the first 14-year-old to get mad at his parents and want to run away.

To get a better sense of the years leading up to his departure, I interviewed several people who lived with Sam and Minnie. While we can only guess what happened, the Katzes enjoyed warm and close relationships with their other children for the rest of their lives. I prefer to think that Isadore was simply restless and bored, and hit a point of no return in his journey where going home would have been too difficult.

Upon discovering his whereabouts, one of my biggest regrets was that Isadore's parents and siblings never found out what happened to him. While it's possible that he may have contacted them at some point, people who knew his parents say that his disappearance was a source of grief and mystery for decades.

I took comfort from the notion that if spirits exist in the afterlife, then they really *did* know what took place, at least from the time of their own deaths onward. That's what inspired the final chapter of this story.

The lives of Isadore and John were as different as they could possibly be, but their souls were really one and the same. Two men, one soul.

If John's entire life flashed before his eyes in 1980, then Isadore must have stood in front of his childhood house just one more time.

Surely his parents and siblings were there to greet him.

Dedicated to my great-grandparents, Sam and Minnie

Sam, Minnie and Grandson Richard, circa 1933

Minnie and the author, 1957

About the Author

Michael Schoenholtz spent 25 years as an information technology executive for large multinational firms. He has travelled extensively throughout the US and the world, both for work and pleasure. Since leaving his corporate career, his primary vocation has been commercial photography. His hobbies include genealogy, travel and gardening.

Michael lives with his family in Portland, Oregon.

He's not embarrassed to admit that this is his first novel.

CPSIA information can be obtained
at www.ICGtesting.com
Printed in the USA
LVHW111536260721
693697LV00017B/873